WHERE THERE ARE MOUNTAINS

SARAH F. PEARLMAN

DEDICATION

To Those Who Came Before...
and...
After

IN MEMORIAM

Carol Capizzi…Roseanne Bilodeau…Lily Cincone

You are missed.

TABLE OF CONTENTS

who will wake us
who will wake us
who will wake us from our
trance of ages
if we don't

    —Judy Grahn,
      "Beauty, sleeping (Who shall wake us)"

PROLOGUE

You say there are no words to describe this time, you say it does not exist.
But remember. Make an effort to remember. Or, failing that, invent.

— Monique Willig
Les Guérillères (1971)

Seven thousand years ago. 5000 BCE. Hunter-gatherers were beginning to live in settlements, planting wild grasses in nearby fields. Grasses that would become grain. It was a time of great migrations. Migrations that took place over hundreds of years and thousands of miles as numerous tribes left the cold and hunger of their northern homelands to travel a path south.

Most were peaceful, wanting only a place where there was food and warmth—struggling past tribes that lived near Mount Olympus and the mountain passes of what would become Hellas. Greece. A matrilineal people that worshiped a female divinity. An Earth Goddess. Celebrating and giving gratitude for the fertility of the land, the birthing of children, and sexual pleasure. Desire without rules.

Others on the path were warrior people. Tribes who came to conquer and enslave. Bringing their male gods.

PART ONE

PART ONE ⚜ CHAPTER 1

THE CAVE

Two skeletons in a sexual embrace.

Leila looked at her half-packed suitcase. Three days ago she had been ready to leave. She was tired. Weary of the heat and stinging insects. Sifting through endless piles of Pelion earth and dirt embedded in fingernails that no amount of washing would remove. She wanted to be home. Back with Rachel. But that was three days ago. Before the cave.

Leila's interest, from the very beginning of graduate training in archeology, was in early Neolithic settlements. At first, in what had been Yugoslavia. Then came the war and all excavations stopped. But she was fortunate enough to receive a grant that connected her to the American Archeological Institute in Athens and obtain a permit to excavate in Greece. And she fell in love with Greece. Its incredible beauty. And mythic past.

But it was the Pelion. That odd peninsula of forested cliffs, lush woodlands, and silver-green olive groves spilling down to the rough sands of the Aegean shore that captured her imagination. A land just south of the mountain passes of Olympus—passes that allowed the massive migrations of prehistoric tribes seeking to escape the barren steppes and freezing cold of what eventually became northern Russia. The Pelion and its legends of centaurs, competitive goddesses, Trojan warriors—and islands with towns named after Mytilini and Myrina. Amazon queens. A land evoking an uncanny sense of familiarity that was hard to comprehend.

Each summer for the past three years, Leila returned to excavate the scatter of Neolithic settlements that dotted the Pelion hillsides. They were not difficult to locate, but there were few findings. Findings that might have told more of the story of the ancient people that had lived there thousands of years ago. Yet she, together with a handful of local workmen, continued to explore the area— digging up the usual pieces of pottery—many etched with a *V* shape that Leila thought represented the beak of a bird.

The summer was ending and they were about to close the dig when a sudden cloudburst became a torrential downpour and then, a steady rain. An avalanche of mud crashed down the Pelion hillside, dislodging trees, boulders, and everything else in its path—including much of the excavation site. Luckily, most of the findings had been wrapped and sent to a museum in nearby Volos. But she and her team of workmen had barely enough time to flee to the nearest village. The roads were impassable and they were forced to stay in a local hotel for more than a week, confined to small rooms without power. The smell of damp clothes and mold everywhere.

When they were finally able to return, the dig was half-buried. But a wealth of arrow heads, bead jewelry, and broken pottery had surfaced—the outcome of flood and upturned earth. And, an almost intact pitcher shaped like a woman with the head of a bird—along with a small number of tiny clay statuettes of females with bird-like heads. Leila called them the Pelion Venuses. Goddesses. Naming the ancient people who had crafted them, the Bird people. Most exciting was a small statuette of two women joined together. Dimi, the head workman, insisted they were Demeter and Persephone. But to Leila, they were identical to the twin goddesses of ancient Anatolia—confirming contact across the Aegean Sea.

They had finally closed the site when Leila heard Dimi shouting. "A *spilaio*. A cave. On the hillside. Next to the olive trees. Right above us."

It took three days. Three days of back-breaking digging, scraping, and brushing away centuries of Pelion rocks and underbrush that had masked the cave. A cave with an opening just large enough to reveal a scattering of bones. Cheers and applause filled the air as they continued to dig until the opening was large enough to enter.

Leila was slightly claustrophobic. She didn't like caves, but she wanted to be the first to see what was inside. Dimi handed her a camera and a helmet with an attached headlight. She put on a mask, knee pads, and gloves, and crawled in. The cave was cold, dank. The ceiling much too low for her to stand and her mask gave little protection from an overpowering stench that brought on waves of nausea.

Before her were two skeletons facing each other. Female from the size of their skulls and shape of their pelvises. Skeletons, not fossils. Close by, and half-buried, was a broken cup-like container with the same inverted *V* as the artifacts found at the dig — suggesting that the women may have lived around 5000 BCE — and perhaps inhabited one of the Pelion settlements. Also, half-buried, was a small triangular stone, faintly etched with lines that she could not quite make out. And what looked like two arrow heads.

Leila took multiple photos of the cave, the skeletons, and the artifacts from every possible angle. Then, she crawled back out. Ripping off her mask. Gagging, trying not to vomit. Gulping in the cool sea air. Thinking what she had to do next.

First, she would need to contact the local archeological council, then fill out multiple government forms and write lengthy reports on what she had found. After that, she could begin negotiations with the Greek archeological authorities as to where the skeletons might be displayed. And request a forensic team to obtain samples of teeth and bones, extract DNA — if possible — and conduct the various tests that would confirm sex, determine their age, the time when they had lived, and the cause of death. But what brought the women to the cave, who they were, and what their lives had been like would remain unknown. Left to Leila's imagination. In the meantime, the cave would have to be guarded; protected from visitors and thieves until a locked gate could be installed.

There was also the possibility of digging deeper into the cave and perhaps finding even more skeletal remains and artifacts. That is, if she could obtain additional excavation permits and funding — assuring her future as an archeologist for a long time to come. And perhaps open up a new chapter on prehistoric Greece. It was an archeologist's dream. Leila's dream. But all she could feel was a pervasive feeling of sadness that she could not ignore. Or understand.

Once back in her room, Leila showered and changed into clean clothes. She opened her laptop, downloaded and enlarged a picture of the small stone. A faint drawing of a woman, perhaps pregnant, with folded arms appeared that surprisingly resembled goddess statuettes excavated in northern Russia and Siberia. Then, after staring at the image of the two skeletons, she began to reconstruct them into life-like, flesh-covered three-dimensional people.

Gradually, two women positioned side-by-side, appeared on the screen. Two women in a sexually intimate embrace. Arms wrapped about each other, one woman's leg between the others. Mouths nearly touching. Leila wasn't able to rotate the figures, but she could see that their profiles showed very different facial features.

Embracing skeletons had been found in Greece before. But they were female and male and buried in tombs. No females who had died embracing one another had ever been unearthed. In the Pelion, or elsewhere. Returning home was now out of the question. She had to remain in Greece, hoping that she could prevent mislabeling by conservative museum officials. And argue against any decision that would result in concealing the skeletons in the recesses of some museum basement. But she feared she was powerless. Whatever was excavated in Greece belonged to Greece.

She needed to talk to Rachel.

Rachel picked up immediately to hear Leila crying.

"What's going on? Are you okay?"

"I'm okay. Listen. You won't believe what we found."

Leila told her about the cave and the two female skeletons locked in an embrace.

"Leila. That's incredible. But you're crying."

"Yes. It's incredible."

Leila tried to explain. The strange connection. The haunting sense of familiarity that drew her to the land.

Rachel listened, trying to understand.

"There's more."

"What?"

"Rachel, whatever is found in Greece belongs to Greece. The decision is theirs. The skeletons aren't acceptable. I'm afraid. No museum will display them. Two women, two skeletons in a sexual embrace? Women lovers? It can't happen. This is Greece. It's just not done."

Rachel was silent, then she asked, "What are you going to do?"

"I don't know. I'll contact the Institute in Athens. Maybe they'll have some suggestions. Some influence. But I think one possibility is that the bones will be taken from the cave and reassembled separately. Displayed separately."

"Leila, I'm so sorry. That's awful."

"Yes, awful."

"When will you be home?"

"I don't know. I have to see what happens."

"You can publish. Talk at conferences."

"Yes. Later on. But now I have to stay."

"Okay. I got it. I understand. Come home soon. Missing you."

"Me too."

Leila put down the receiver and looked out her window. On one side were hillsides reaching up to the Pelion mountains. On the other, an arbor of purple grapes nestled in green leaves. And then the Aegean shore. Tears filled her eyes. But it wasn't sadness or sorrow that she felt. It was grief.

PART TWO

THE PATH

They had been traveling for so long that not one was alive to remember the land of their origin. Only stories to tell the tale. Then the war people came and the stories were forgotten.

There was not a sound. Not one sound that could have told us they were near. Only soft winds and the rustling of leaves. The stirring of a nearby brook. The buzzing of insects. It was a long time before I let myself remember. And an even longer time before I let myself tell another person.

We were traveling south, following a path made by people long gone. One of many tribes escaping the dying steppes. Fleeing famine and the freezing cold. Travel was slow and hunger and exhaustion with us much of the time. And, the heat of sun-scorched summers bringing thirst and stinging insects. But the hardest were the stretches of land, yellow with dust, making it even more of a struggle to find food. And the cold times that had us huddle, shivering in blankets—the mountain passes blocked by snow. Calling on *Ge*, our Goddess, to help us survive.

Sometimes the path would wander in-between cliffs, or take us to the foothills of mountains. Many times it was narrow, carved through thick forests. Other times, it nearly disappeared and was no more than trampled underbrush. Then, it would become wide again — and when the air warmed — bordered by fields of green grass and flowers in bloom. We went wherever the path took us. Walking until we could walk no longer and hunger demanded that we find food. Then, we would struggle to walk even further until we reached woodlands and would make our way away from the trail to find a place to rest for the night.

But first, we would heap underbrush and tree branches behind us to conceal that we had left the path. Scattered bones along the way told that it was unsafe and could bring death to those who followed it. Many tribes were traveling south. Some were men on horses with sharp spears and arrows. We called them the *Tardos*. War people. Like the Kurgas or the Vlamas. Tribes that killed for food and animal skins. And women.

If we were fortunate, we would find water and a cave to shelter us — some with odd people and animals painted on their walls. Or, an overhang of a cliff. We would gather nuts and fruits in the woodlands and hunt for game. And, if there was a nearby stream, catch fish. Then, when darkness came, made fires for cooking and warmth — and to keep the hungry animals away. Eat what food we had, spread our cloaks on the ground and sleep, wrapped in damp blankets — returning to the path the next day. Or the next. The only life I knew.

The happiest of times were when we would find a clearing in the woodlands and make a camp to stay longer. Long enough to gather yellow grasses to pound into grain for flatcakes, dig up roots, and set traps to catch small animals. And Maija, my mother's sister, would add herbs to flavor our soups and stews, and berries to sweeten the flatcakes. Sometimes, food was so plentiful, so abundant — mostly, when we had killed a large animal — that we did not have to gather, or hunt during the days that followed. But eventually, we would pack up and return to the path — and, once again, begin the journey south. To a place called the *Ilios*, the Sunlands. The *Ilios*, where we were told food was plentiful, hunger would no longer follow us, and the sun shone all year. This is what our stories said.

Other times, we would make a more permanent camp and stay for two, three, or four full moons. Mostly when there was illness among us, or a woman was about to birth. Or, when the cold times were about to begin, bringing ice and snow. We would build huts from tree bark and underbrush. Hunt. Set traps. Pound animal skins until they were soft enough to make into blankets and cloaks to protect us from sharp winds. Salt meat to last through the cold times. And to bring when we returned to the path. There was always work to be done. Mending boots, sewing tunics, making pouches, slings, spears, bows and arrows. But we did not mind. We were in no hurry to leave. The *Ilios*, the Sunlands, could wait.

When the days became warm again, we returned to the path. Yet, there was beauty and wonder as we traveled south. Flower-covered fields perfumed the air with their sweet scent—accompanying us as we walked. Orange-gold sunsets spreading across the sky. A half-moon hovering over a mountain peak. Stars decorating the blackness of night. And once, as we passed a stretch of low mountains, we heard a frightening noise that deafened our ears and saw a great water crashing down a cliff. We ran, climbing upwards, slipping on wet rocks until we reached a ledge behind the falling water. There, we bathed and danced in its mists until the sky darkened, telling us we had to return to the path.

At nightfall, we would light our fires, laugh, joke, tell stories, share dreams. And play games and sing. My uncle, Maija's brother, Aran, would breathe music into a reed pipe—making sounds that spoke of yearning, bringing me to tears. But I did not know what I yearned for.

And we would dance. Dance to the sound of reed pipes and gourds made with strings stretched tight. Whenever there was music, we would dance. Sometimes in circles. Whirling about until we were light-headed. Rolling our hips as if we were *erojai*. Lovers. Love-making. Mimicking women rubbing against women, or men entering a woman. Or animals mounting each other.

Then, during each full moon, all of us would gather to thank *Ge*. Singing our gratitude for the caves that sheltered us, the woodlands and streams that fed us, and the animals that clothed and nourished us. Celebrating the birth of children and the melting feelings of desire that would spread throughout our bodies. Making us shake and bringing us to a joyous shudder. Praising Her until sleep would take us.

We were the Naorji. Twenty in number. Too small a group to walk the path safely and so we had joined with another tribe on the way south. Now we were thirty. Only thirty. So many of us had died. From the freezing cold. Starvation. Illness. Hungry animals. Sometimes, a woman from birthing. But we were still a joyous people. Even though there were many hardships and we were far from the *Ilios*, the Sunlands.

My mother was long dead. I slept close to Maija. And her son, Miko. He was perhaps six winters. A small boy for his years. I was my mother's first daughter and had been given her mother's name. Yanija. My *awija*, my grandmother's name. So no one would be forgotten. My mother had birthed a second daughter and I would have had a sister, but she did not live.

I questioned Maija many times. Why were we following the path. Why could we not stay where the gathering was good and there were brooks and streams filled with fish.

Her answers were short. "It is foretold," she would say. Or, "It is our fate."

Then I would ask her, once again, where our homeland was. Why we had left. Why was it taking so long and how will we know when we reach the *Ilios*, the Sunlands.

She said, "I was born on the path. Same as my mother and grandmother. And others before them. Our home was north. Far, far north. No animals to hunt. Empty traps. No fish to catch. Hunger. Many people left before us. Other tribes went after. That is why we left. Why we follow the path south. To run. To run from the cold and dust that follow. Many times, we would make a camp and stay for three, sometimes four, warming or cold times. Hoping we had found a new home. But then, the cold and ice would find us. Once again, less to gather. No animals to hunt. No fish to catch. And so we would return to the path.

"How will we know when we reach the *Ilios*, the Sunlands? We will know when we see a sea so great that large lands will float upon it."

Then she said, "Yanija, I am not unhappy. I do not like the cold times, or when hunger is with us. But it brings me happiness to walk the path. To see what lies ahead. To watch the mountains change.

Green, when the warming time greets us. Capped with snow and ice when the cooling time begins. Some with jagged tops like an animal's teeth. Others nearly covered by mist. One mountain behind another. Another mountain behind that mountain. Then another. Endless."

This is what Maija said. And, I began to watch the mountains.

I was perhaps fourteen winters. Many full moons past my first blood. I was no longer a *korwah*, a young girl, and I had my first entering. With a boy from the other tribe. Although it was more curiosity than desire. I did like the feeling of him inside me. But I liked girls better. Girls who knew where to put fingers and tongues.

Like all of my tribe, the Naorji, I could use sticks and small pieces of wood to make fire. Trap small animals, find the nests of birds that gave us eggs, dig up roots, and gather herbs in the woodlands to flavor our stews. I had learned the skill of plant healing and knew which leaves, when squeezed, would release its juices and heal infection and wounds. And others, that when women were birthing a child, could quiet the pain. I knew each one's name, their purpose by the shape of their leaves, their scent, color, or taste. Some were bitter. Others rough. Still others were soft. Like the petals of a flower. And Maija had taught me how to sew beads on the small pouches that I carried in my sack. Each one decorated with a different design to tell what was inside.

But I could never learn to use a sling, or shoot arrows. Or throw a spear. And often missed whatever I was aiming at. Maija said my eyes were crooked. Yet, I knew the trees that gave us *leino*. Flax for ropes and belts and I could find the tree bark that, when boiled in water, would bring on a woman's bleeding time after a man had entered her. And the small white berries that made a tiny infant leave its mother's body if she did not want to birth.

I knew the trees that shielded the different plants. One, surrounded by moist Earth, told that certain plants were near. Others hid under trees that grew in dry soil. Still others crouched beneath small bushes. And some opened their leaves only when the woodlands became dark. Then, fearful of the large cats that hunted by night, we would search the forest with small torches, returning quickly with great relief to our camp.

The woodlands gave us everything we needed. Water, food, oil from seeds. Juices that, when pressed from plant leaves and mixed with ashes from our fires, would cleanse our hair and bodies. And the tiny pointed stalks that grew close to Earth and made breath fragrant.

It was Yula who was the oldest of our tribe. Our *Agetes*. Our leader. The only one with hair turning white. Yula, unlike Maija, was impatient, argumentative. But, at times, she let me accompany her into the woodlands. She would say very little and acted like she thought I was a nuisance. But once, she stopped and pointed to an odd-looking plant. She was laughing, a gurgling sound, as she squeezed the liquid out of its leaves.

She said, "Keep this to make insects go away. Or, if you do not want to take a man into you."

Its scent was vile, but still I thought she was joking. No man would enter a woman unless she desired him.

Yula would squeeze out juice from rotting fruit, then pour the liquid into a jug. Days later, she would give us small amounts to swallow—warming us inside and making us laugh and dance, and *eroja*i, love-make, with even more abandon. Other times, she would throw certain leaves on our fires and we would breathe in its smoke. Smoke that brought us dreams and visions. Yula knew where to find the ragged circles that grew close to wet Earth when we needed to hear messages from *Ge*. And which plants, if eaten, could cause illness, even death. And it was Yula who could foretell the future times by watching how the clouds moved about in the sky. But the clouds did not tell that a war tribe was coming.

It was the end of the cold times and, once again, we were preparing to return to the path. It was a good day. A day of sun. Not a cloud in the sky. Miko had followed me into the nearby woodlands, helping to search for nuts, berries, and grasses to fill my sack. Maija had taught me and now I was the one to teach. To show Miko the plants that added flavor to food, those that grew leaves to suck on when thirsty, and another that could be eaten when hungry.

But what he liked best was to empty my pouch to see what was inside. A few dried berries, a small gourd to catch water, a bone needle and thread, flint and sticks to make fires, sharp arrow heads for spears, my knife—and my precious small stone—etched with a likeness of *Ge*. For protection and good fortune.

I heard not a sound. Just the woodland breezes. Miko was hanging my sack and cloak on a low tree branch while I knelt by a stream, watching for small fish. I was enjoying the chill of the water when suddenly I heard shouting, screaming. The war cry, *Alala*. And then, he was there. Hair tangled and dirty. Face streaked with black paint. A boy really, but big. I was small.

I tried to run, but he stopped me. Punching at my face, throwing me on the ground, ripping off my skirt. Forcing himself into me. I did not understand. I did not know a man could do this. Among my people, before a woman would take a man into her, he would bow his head between her legs. Giving gratitude. Honoring the place of birth and pleasure.

I passed from Earth because of the pain from his plunging. When I awoke, I saw his face. A beautiful face. But cold eyes. Eyes without light. Dead eyes. He turned me over. Crushing my leg, holding my head up by my hair. Something sharp slashed across my throat. And slashed again. Then he was gone.

Weeping, I half lay in the stream. The water swirling, turning red as blood poured out. I tried to press my tunic against my throat to quiet the bleeding, but I passed from Earth again. Then, Miko was there. Crouching by my side. Pale. Dirty. Eyes unseeing, glancing past me. I did not know where he had hid, or what he had seen. I tried to speak, but I had no voice. The man's knife had taken my voice. And Miko could not speak. Fear had taken his voice.

It seemed like a long time before he finally understood my gestures and brought my pouch and sack so I could find the leaves to stop the bleeding. And then, my cloak and skirt. And spear. I dared not move because of weakness. And pain. My leg hurt badly. One eye was swollen and it was difficult to see. I felt a great pain on the side of my face where the man had punched me. Another pain was inside me from his plunging and a terrible pain where he had slashed at me. I slowly removed my tunic from my throat and the bleeding began again. But I found the leaves in my sack that healed wounds and they stopped most of it. All but a trickle.

More time passed before I was able to stand. Leaning on
Miko, I took off my blood-stained tunic and, together, we buried
it in the ground. Fearful that the scent of blood would bring hungry animals. I washed as best as I could and covered myself with
my cloak. And with his help, limped slowly back to the camp. So
many bodies. I did not want to look, but I saw two of my kinsmen
lying dead. One was Aran, Maija's brother. His head crushed.
Little was left. The *Tardos* had set fire to our tents. Taken our
carts, animal hides, food. Miko hid in the woodlands. He would
not enter the camp.

Maija was gone. Yula and Aran and Aran's music were gone.
The Naorji, my tribe, were gone. I did not know if any had escaped,
or were taken. Fearful the men would return, Miko and I made our
way to a nearby cliff to hide among the rocks. Then, when darkness came, we lit a fire to keep the animals away. I could not chew
the berries we had gathered, but squeezed out their juices that, in
spite of the pain, I made myself swallow. We tried to sleep, huddled
together in my cloak. But rustling leaves and animal sounds kept
us awake. And fear. When the sun rose, we waited. Waited, hoping
that someone from our tribe would appear. But no one did.

I still could not speak the next day, nor walk that well. Miko
did not speak. His voice had left, but I made him understand he had
to find food—gesturing that he go back to the stream to catch fish.
When he returned, I made a soup that I could drink. And, again,
we waited. Waited for three days. I knew I should have felt grief.
But grief takes many forms and sometimes hides. I was distracted
by pain. And fear left no room for sorrow.

I sent Miko off the next day to find more food. This time he did
not return. I waited, thinking that perhaps he was lost and would
find his way back. I searched the nearby woodlands as best I could,
but I had seen the last of him. Perhaps it was an animal. There
were still large cats about. I tried to keep those thoughts away. And
thoughts that it was my fault since I was the one who had sent him
for food. That would come later.

I felt no sadness. Nor did I make tears. There was only fear. And
very little food. I knew I could not survive alone. That I would die. I
was still in pain. Weak and could barely walk. But I knew the way back

to the path. I waited until the next day's light to give myself enough time until darkness came. Then, leaning on my spear and carrying my sack, I began to make my way. Stopping many times to rest. Fearful that a hungry animal or the war people would come back and find me. My only hope was to reach the path before nightfall and that it would not be too long before another tribe passed and would take me in. I could have ended my life, but the will to live is strong.

I did not know if I found them. Or, if they found me. I had stopped close to the path, leaning against a tree because of weakness, and suddenly they were there. A small group of people surrounding me. Perhaps fifteen in all. Nearly all women. I could not speak, but make only rasping sounds as I tried to tell them my tribe had been attacked and all, except myself, were dead. Or taken. But not what the man had done to me. From the look on their faces, I knew I must have been quite a sight. I could only guess what the wounds on my throat and my chin looked like. But they were a kind people and took me with them.

They were the Aziri. Another tribe traveling the path south. They saw I was too weak to make the journey and so they made a camp and cared for me. Bathing my wounds to stop infection. Placing healing leaves on my throat and chin. Preparing foods that I could swallow. And one woman, Tani, gave me a tunic and mended my skirt.

Tani became my close friend. Although her people's talk was different from that of my tribe, there were many words I could understand. But I could not speak. Only watch and listen. I saw they were a serious people. A quiet people. Not like my tribe, the Naorji. They did not sing or dance at nightfall. And they told few stories. But they did give praise to a Goddess they called, *Yah*. The same Goddess as ours. Just a different name.

It took me time to push out the words, but I managed to ask why there were so few men. Tani answered, saying the *Tardos*, the war people, had attacked them and many were killed or wounded.

She said, "The *Tardos* went after the men. Perhaps they thought, that without the men, they could take us. The women. But Aziri women fight. And so we fought them off. Though most of our men had been killed. Only two left.

"After that, the fever illness came and more of us left Earth. So much death. My mother and my sister. Many children. And the woman I was with. All happiness left my people, the Aziri,. Now we are fifteen. Only fifteen. A tribe of women."

I could not speak long. Only whisper. I waited a while, then took her hand and said, "What did I look like when you first saw me?"

Tani hesitated, then replied, "One eye was badly swollen. Your face was covered with bruises turning blue and we saw dried blood on your throat and chin. We did not think you would live."

The next day I told her, once again, how the war people had attacked us. Whispering, I asked her who they were. Why they killed. Why they took women.

Tani thought for a while, then said, "Hunger. Hunger brings anger. Sometimes will make you kill for food. Perhaps the *Tardos* were hungry and learned to kill. To take. Now they live by killing and taking."

"Why do they take women? What happens to the women they take?"

"They become *dolos*. Slaves."

She saw I did not understand and said, "They belong to the men."

I still did not understand.

"They belong. Like your pouch. A belonging. Used for work. For entering. Taking the children you birth to make more people for their tribe."

It was then I understood.

Tani helped me to sew a scarf from a piece of animal skin that hid the wounds on my chin and throat. But my voice did not return and I could never really speak again. Only whispering and slowly rasping out words. I knew I was disfigured. No woman would ever want me. Nor any man. It did not matter. I had no desire. My voice was gone. Desire was gone. Desire for a woman—or a man—was gone.

Like all of the tribes traveling south, the Aziri were skilled gatherers and healers. They knew many herbs and plants, but others were strange to them. I wanted to be of value and, as I grew stronger, I showed them the places in the woodlands where one could find the different plant leaves that fed hunger and quenched thirst.

And the herbs that flavored stews and flatcakes. And so the Aziri became my people.

When I could walk without limping, we returned to the path. And my life of traveling south began again. Long days of walking, then seeking a place to rest when darkness came. Like my people, the Naorji, the Aziri were hoping to join with another tribe as they were too small in number to be safe. But this did not happen.

I soon found I was with child and feared it was because of the man who had slashed my throat and taken my voice. Too late to rid myself of it safely, I swore to myself, if it was a boy, I would kill him. If it was a girl and she had the man's face, I would kill her. It was only when I could feel the child stir within me that I was able to cry. And I wept for my people. For Maija. Aran. For Yula. And for Miko. Especially Miko. It was then I told Tani what the man had done to me and that it was I who had sent Miko to his death. Tani held me while I wept. And she wept along with me.

I birthed a girl and she did not have his face. Her face was like my mother's face. She had my people's face and, at times, I thought I saw the smile of the boy who had first entered me. This daughter reached my heart and I loved her from the moment she was birthed. I named her, Ayala. Gift. After my mother.

Ayala brought a new happiness to the Aziri people. Few children had been born and those who were birthed had not lived long. Everyone wanted to hold her. To make her smile and hear her sweet laughing noises. She was so loved by them. Loved by so many people, I knew she would be strong. And my breasts gave much milk and she thrived. Now I walked the path with my child cradled in a shawl wrapped around my body.

Tani loved to talk and told many stories. Stories her mother and grandmother had told to her. About her people traveling the path and how they had once reached a great sea. A sea without end. And Tani said the stories told that they had met up with a tribe, called the *Tektai*, who lived along its shore. A people who would lie on the sand when the sun was high in the sky — and walk into the water — kicking their legs and waving their arms so they became like fish. I had walked into the waters of different lakes and streams, sometimes up to my waist. But becoming like a fish was hard to believe.

Then Tani said the *Tektai* would hollow out trees and make them into gourds. Long gourds that they would bring into the sea. Then, they would climb inside, bringing sticks that moved them through the water. Sometimes so far out you could no longer see them. And then they would return, bringing back fish as large as children.

All I could do was nod in amazement.

"Yes. Food was plentiful near the great sea. There were animals to hunt, fish to catch, and much to gather in the nearby woodlands. We, the Aziri, would have left the path and made the shore our new home. But other tribes were passing and told that the war people were near. And so we left the *Tektai* and the great water and returned to the path."

These were the stories that Tani's mother and grandmother had told to her. Other stories were about the *Synkalos*, the Great Gatherings, where people from the many tribes traveling the path south would meet in a clearing near the woodlands. To dance, sing, trade bead jewelry and animal skins. To share knowledge about where to find food and how to travel the path safely. And all would praise our Mother Goddess who had many names. Then laughing, Tani added that sounds of pleasure would be heard all through the darkness of nightfall and, many full moons later, children would be birthed.

I had been to the *Synkalos* and heard the moans and sounds of pleasure that lasted throughout the night. I knew the women who went into the woodlands with women, those who went with men, and the men who sought to be with other men. And the women who liked women, but went with men when they wanted to birth a child. I would hear the sounds of pleasure and my fingers would go between my legs. Moving until a melting feeling entered my body and I shuddered with delight. But that was then.

I did ask Tani about the woman she was with.

Her face became sad as she replied. "Her name was Sogi. But I do not speak of her."

"You do not speak of the dead?"

"We speak of the dead. But I do not speak of her."

It was three, nearly four, cold times when a war tribe came again. This time on the path. Men on horses. A different tribe. Not the *Tardos* who had killed my people. I had stopped to give Ayala my milk, but they found us. Surrounded us. Ayala began to wail and, fearful they would do us harm, I took her to my breast to quiet her. I did not understand their language, but from their gestures, I knew what they wanted to do to me. I took off my scarf so they could see the scars on my throat and chin. It was my disfigured face that saved me. Saved me from the men who wanted to drink from my breasts. From those who wanted to force themselves into me.

I never knew what happened to Tani. Or the others. If they had been killed, or if they had escaped. The war people took me and my child. At first, I did not know why. But I soon understood it was for the milk in my breasts. For the infants whose mothers could not nurse. They found two other Aziri women hiding in the woodlands and took them as well.

The two women died shortly after we returned to the path. What happened to them, I did not know. And, once again, I was too afraid to grieve. There was no time for sorrow. I had to prove my worth once my milk stopped. Thinking they might kill me or Ayala. Or leave us behind on the path to die.

I gathered the herbs that flavored stews and the plant leaves that healed wounds, pounded the grasses that would become flatcakes, and salted the meat from the animals the men had killed. But I concealed the leaves that would bring on a woman's bleeding time, the small white berries that made an infant leave the womb long before birth, the ones that brought on sleep, and those that caused death. And I hid Yula's plant leaves that gave off the terrible stench.

And so my third life began. Back on the path. But a much harder life. A terrible life. There were so many of them. Too many to count. Many tents. Many fires at nightfall. The men had broad shoulders, their bodies covered with light hair. Brutal men who screamed, cursed, and quarreled constantly. And fought one another. Some more vicious than others. They were unlike any people I had ever known. Taller than the women which was strange. The women and men I had lived with, the Naorji and the Aziri, were all the same size. At first, I thought they were the Kurgas. Or the Vlamas. But then I heard them say they were the Zsuirai. It did not matter.

It was only the men who hunted. Only the men who rode horses. Not the women. Only the men who went ahead to see what was before us on the path. Sometimes they returned with bead jewelry and animal skins and I knew they had attacked another tribe.

Tani had told me about *dolos*. Slaves. But I did not truly understand until I was with these people. The women were slaves. Cowering, frightened women. Speaking to each other only when the men were away. Quiet, silent when they returned. Nearly all were bruised. From beatings. Used for cooking, gathering, mending, and building huts when we made camp before the cold times came. And for entering. Some by many men.

It was Ayala who learned the Zsuirai language. I did not. Only a few words. But to survive, I observed their ways. Before sleep, the men would meet to plan the next day. And, sometimes dance and sing. How they danced was strange. Just jumping and turning. A few of the women jumped. Others just watched. Most odd was that they gave thanks, not to a Goddess, but to a man. Someone they called *Hjis*. I did not know why they gave thanks to him. Perhaps for killing. For plunder. Certainly not for birthing a child.

I made no friendships with the other women. I was alone with my daughter. Sleeping in tents or huts on the edge of their camps. Ayala, once full of joy and laughter, became a fearful child. A quiet child. Frightened when I was not near. If it were not for her, I would have escaped to the woodlands. Taken my chances. But I could not leave because of Ayala. I could have killed myself, but I could not die because if I died, Ayala would die. I had to live so Ayala would live.

It was my tribe, the Naorji, who had kept me alive. Then, the Aziri. I was Naorji, but I did not know who I was without my people. Now, I had no tribe and because I had no tribe, I had to use all my fierceness to keep Ayala alive. I was now my child's tribe and I had to live long enough to teach her how to survive. How to gather, set traps, heal wounds, salt meat. To keep her from becoming a Zsuirai. And long enough for her to grow and reach the age when she would understand what must be concealed. Kept secret.

But it was with the Zsuirai that Ayala grew. Then, as she began to leave her child-age, I saw she was ashamed of me. Ashamed of how I looked. She wanted to belong. But we were taken. We were not Zsuirai. Then, as she approached her first bleeding, I saw the men watching her and knew that one, or another, would take her. I had watched carefully and saw that some of the women were protected by belonging to one man. Those who were not protected could be used, entered by any man. And so I watched. Watched for a man who would protect her. One that she would belong to. A man who would not give her to other men.

Gerik was what he was called. He was really only a boy. Not much older than Ayala. I saw that he could not take his eyes off her. That he would sometimes help her gather wood for fires. Find reasons to be around her. That she made him smile. He was slow. Not quick and there was no way I could know, but I hoped he would be kind. Unlike the other Zsuirai men. That he would protect her. Not give her to other men. At least for a time. And so I began to talk to Ayala about Gerik. But I waited to whisper about escape.

PART TWO ⚜ CHAPTER 3

AYALA

Where will I go? Who will I go to?

Ever since I had memory, my life was traveling the path south. Struggling to keep up with the carts and the men on horseback. Keeping my mother in sight as she walked, bent over by the animal skins and food she carried. Making our way—from sunrise until nearly dark—up and down hills, across lowlands, or through the mountain passes. Then, when darkness came, seek a place to camp. Or sleep on the path. My mother and I. Our blankets and cloaks on wet ground. The stars above. Each day like the one before.

Always exhausted. Always seeking food. Trying to escape the cold. And always there was disagreement and fighting among the men. A hard life. A life with little happiness. I knew no other life. We lived traveling to a place my mother called the *Ilios*, the Sunlands.

Many times we would make a camp in the woodlands for one or two full moons. The men would hunt and the women gather and set traps so that there would be food to eat, or bring with us when we were back on the path. Sometimes we would remain longer, mostly during the cold times. And twice, because of the fever illness, we stayed in one place for three warming times before we returned, once again, to the path.

My mother, Yanija, was Naorji. Not Zsuirai. Always at my side. Whether on the path, or while gathering or trapping. To be certain I was safe. Protected. At nightfall, before sleep, I would lay, curled in her arms, and she would whisper stories. Ever since I was a small child. She told me many times the *Tardos*, a war people, had attacked her tribe and a man had cut her throat and chin. Leaving her alive, but without a voice. Only whispering and rasping noises. Her throat and chin were badly scarred and she would wind a long scarf around her head and neck to conceal her wounds.

"We were caught off guard," she said. "And that was the end of us. I think I was the only one to survive. Now you and I, we are the last of the Naorji. No more."

Then she would tell me how another tribe, the Aziri, had taken her in and it was there that she birthed me. We lived with them for perhaps four cold times. But that was before I had memory. Then they, too, were attacked. This time by the Zsuirai who took us. My mother and I. This is what she would tell me.

The Zsuirai avoided my mother. Mocked her. The women and the men. They would call her *probos*. Ugly face. Yet, it was her they sought to heal wounds, cure those who were ill with the fever sickness, or help a woman birth a child. They insulted her, but they seemed afraid of her. As if she had special powers. She also had the gift of making food delicious. Adding certain dried herbs to the flatcakes and stews. Rubbing them on meat roasting on cooking fires. I think we might have been killed, or left behind, if she did not have these skills. And so they let us live.

I was a lonely child. There were few girl children and they, like the Zsuirai women and men, taunted my mother. I did have one friend, but only for a short time. A sad girl called Eta. She was older, but we would keep each other company as we gathered or mended. She did not have a mother and although I knew the Zsuirai did not speak of the dead, I asked her what had happened

She replied, "She was injured. She could not walk and was left behind. On the path."

I took her hand said, "Eta, I am so sorry. When did this happen?"

She turned her face away. "Perhaps three cold times ago."

It was not long after that she was given to one of the men. And then she rarely spoke to me.

As I grew older, I became ashamed of my mother. I did not want a mother like her. Her scarred throat and chin. Trying to conceal her wounds behind a scarf. A mother who was called *probos*, ugly face so that the other children avoided me. I wanted one who could speak. Not one who could only whisper. A mother who knew the Zsuirai language so I did not have to speak for her. Or, tell her what the Zsuirai spoke about.

I was no longer interested in her stories about people I did not know. Or ancestors without names. Weary of her praising *Ge*. Her Goddess. A Goddess who did not protect us. I did not want to hear her rasping voice telling me about plant leaves and tree barks — and what they could be used for. Nor did I care what she carried in her pouch. And I hated that she always had to be near.

But that was before the Zsuirai men attacked another tribe. This time on the path for all to see. My mother tried to hide me. Covering my eyes and pulling me under her cloak so that I would not know what was happening. What the men were doing. But I heard. The shouting. The screams. The pleading. And I did see. I saw the blood that was everywhere. The bodies without heads. Women. Children. Blood dripping from axes before the men wiped them clean. Hearing them boast about how many they had killed.

My mother and I were shocked. Dazed. I because I had never seen such brutality and bloodshed. My mother because she had seen this before.

Not long after, my mother took me to see two Zsuirai women. Both were badly beaten by the men they had been given to. Faces bruised. Limping. One was Eta. The girl who had been my friend. I tried to speak to her, but she turned away. Ashamed.

Pointing at them, my mother asked, "Is this the life you want? Is this who you want to be? A *dolo*? A slave? A Zsuirai woman?"

It was then that I began to listen. Listen carefully at nightfall as she whispered about her life before the *Tardos* came. About her *Eshar*, her blood kin. Yula, Maija, Aran. And Miko. About the *Synkalos*, the Great Gatherings, where many tribes would meet to trade and celebrate Earth that fed them. The stories she had

heard about their far north homeland and *Ge*, her people's Goddess.
How the Aziri had found her and taken her in. And Tani, the Aziri
woman, who told her about a great sea with fish that were as big
as children.

For the first time since I was a child, I asked where we had
come from. Where our homeland was. Why we were traveling south.

She replied, "I can only say what I was told. The stories that
were passed down. It was long before my mother's time. And my
grandmother's. And my grandmother's mother. We, the Naorji, lived
north. Far north. Floods had drenched the woodlands and there
were other years without rain. And then a great cold. A cold that
followed us everywhere. A cold that brought ice and snow. Hunger,
illness. And death."

She stopped for a while, then began to whisper again. "Those
who were strong enough began to leave. Our tribe, the Naorji, were
among them. Some had gone before us. Others left after. We fled to
make our way south—believing in a sun-lit land strewn with flowers
and trees heavy with fruit. A place near a great water with waves
carrying fish that rolled up on the shore. Nothing like the frozen
steppes that had once been our home. Bringing starvation and early
death. This is what the stories told."

And then her voice left. Gave out as it often did. When it
returned and she was able to whisper once again, I asked how we
would know when we reached the *Ilios*, the Sunlands.

"It will be when we reach a sea so huge that we will see large
lands floating on it."

Then she said, "Ayala, listen. It was not always this way. From
the time I had memory, I saw women hunt. Naorji women hunted.
Aziri women hunted. Women were our leaders. Our *Agetes*. No
woman was beaten. No woman belonged to a man. No woman
would be entered unless it was her wish. No woman was a *dolo*."

I looked at her face. Her wide-set eyes and curled hair—and
knew she had once been beautiful. She held herself straight as if
she were tall. Not like the cowering Zsuirai women. And I began
to watch. Watch carefully as she sought out the different plants
that grew in the woodlands near the path. Watched as she showed
me the shape of their leaves, what they felt like when touched,

their scent, their taste. Leaves that could heal wounds or stop coughs and returned breath. Those that, when sucked, would quench thirst. And another that could take away hunger. I learned where they grew, how to find them, what they could be used for. And their names.

My mother also showed me the plant leaves that had to be kept secret. One brought on a woman's bleeding time when she did not want a child. There were white berries that made a small infant leave a woman's body long before birth and another plant that was poisonous and could bring death. And still another gave off a terrible stench that made us pinch our noses and laugh. Then, she made me a pouch and filled it with plant leaves the same as hers. And taught me how to fit an arrow head on a walking stick so that it became a spear. Even though Zsuirai women were not allowed to use weapons.

I saw how she dried the small leaves that she used to flavor stews and flatcakes and meat roasting on fires and how gifted and useful she was. It was then I understood why we were taken and made to live with the Zsuirai. But I thought that what my mother was teaching me would be my survival. So I would be of worth to the Zsuirai. It was only later I understood she had more in mind.

Right before my first blood, she began to whisper about Gerik. That it would be good if I were given to him. That he would protect me from the other men. I did not want to go to Gerik. There was someone else I liked. A boy with silken hair and dreamy dark eyes who, when I dared look at him, made me feel slightly faint. But there were only looks between us and not many. Just a few.

Gerik took me which I knew was fortunate when I saw the sad face of the girl who had been given to the boy with dreamy eyes. Bruised. Limping. Crying silently. The life, the fate of most Zsuirai women. I knew of women who were beaten so badly that they were left behind on the path to die. Like the ones who were wounded or too ill to continue the journey.

I did not dislike Gerik. He was kind. At first. And he did protect me from the other men. But when I took my attention away from him, he would became sullen, as if he were a child. Or, if he thought I liked another man. He did not beat me. But soon after I was given to him, he began to slap me. Sometimes it was playful and he would laugh as he slapped at me. Other times, it was when he was angry. Mostly, a swat on one ear or the other. But his slapping did hurt and I feared that one day my ears would be injured so badly that I would no longer be able to hear. I did not tell my mother, but I think she knew.

I had no say. Nor did I have any say — or pleasure — when he would push himself inside me. Thrusting. Pounding until a loud grunt told me he was finished. Then, he would roll off me and sleep. On the path at nightfall, or when we made a camp in the woodlands. Each night, unless he was too tired from the day's travel or hunt. In the dawn hours too, unless I woke up before him and slipped away. That was when he would slap at me the most.

The only time I could escape his poundings was during my bleeding time. Or when he was away with the other men on a long hunt, or scouting the path ahead. At times, I would add certain dried herbs to the stews I cooked for him. Herbs that made sleep so that he would leave me alone. Sometimes, I would move my fingers high up between my thighs. But it was more release than pleasure.

His thrusting brought me a daughter who died shortly after I birthed her. I would have had more children, but my mother had taught me how to push a tiny piece of animal skin up inside of me — one soaked in a tea made from dried leaves. Leaves that closed my womb. And I knew how to brew another tea that brought on my bleeding time.

I would have liked a daughter. To be a mother to her like my mother was to me. But I did not mourn long. I did not want a daughter who would live a life like mine. A daughter who would learn to be afraid and cower like the Zsuirai women. I did not want a son. I knew if I birthed a son, he would become like Gerik. Like the other men. Cruel and bullying.

Not long after the death of my child, my mother grew ill from a fever illness. I would sit by her side, stroking her hair, feeding her thin soup and tea. Hoping they would bring her strength. But the sickness would not leave and I knew she would soon die. Just before she left Earth, she tried to speak, but it was difficult to hear her words. I think she was telling me not to trust any Zsuirai woman.

That what I said could be repeated to gain favor with the men. To act uncertain and make light of what I knew so there would be less envy. At least, that is what I thought she was saying.

Then, she made her whispering louder and said, "Ayala, we are nearing the Sunlands. The *Ilios*. The cold is still following us, but the cold times are not as bitter as they once were. The snows are not as deep. It will soon be time for you to leave. To escape."

She had never said these words before. Fear entered my body. "Escape? Where? Where would I go?"

"Yes, escape."

Again, I asked, "Where will I go? Who will I go to?"

She stopped to catch breath, then answered, "You will know. You will find them."

"Who? Who are they? Where will they be?"

"The woodlands. Go to the woodlands."

"The woodlands?"

It was then I understood her insistence that I learn all that she knew about gathering and healing. And making spears. It was not to survive among the Zsuirai. It was to escape from them.

My mother lingered as if she did not want to leave. I could see the pain in her eyes as she struggled to breathe. I held her rough hands — calloused from a lifetime of hard work. Her skin hot to my touch. I told her that I was sorry. Sorry for how I behaved when I was young. But she did not seem to understand. She no longer had the strength to whisper, but could only mouth a few words. Two words.

"Promise me."

I said, "I promise."

I kissed her on the mouth. Above her scarred chin and throat. At the end, she took a breath, then stopped, only to breathe again. Then, she slept and died soon after. I would not leave her on the path and buried her in the woodlands. Gerick helped. At first. But he soon grew impatient and left. I sat, for a time, beside her buried body. Weeping, Thinking about all that she had told me. Memories of her and her stories filled my mind as I held her *Ge* stone in my hands. I thought about escape. I knew of a woman who had tried and been caught. Killed. But not before many men had forced themselves into her. And I became even more afraid. Troubling dreams would wake me in the dark of night. Dreams of being lost in the woodlands. Dreams of hungry animals finding me. I would wake up shaking. My body covered with sweat.

Life went on as before. But lonely. Back on the path. Always on the path. Always seeking food. Always exhausted. Travel was now slow as we climbed up, then down, and up again through mountain passes. Through rain and mud. Sleeping near the path. When we finally reached the lower hills and woodlands, snow began to fall and we stopped to make a camp. A camp where we would stay until the cold times passed.

Gerik was becoming angry. Insistent that I give him a child. Slapping at me. Punching me. Shouting why was I not making him a son. Threatening to give me to other men. But I knew if I had a child, I could never leave. And so, I kept my womb closed. I would feel the bruises on my face, trying not to weep. Thinking of my mother's words. Asking myself, "Am I now a *dolo*? A slave? A Zsuirai woman?"

Then, as the days became warmer, the men began to leave the camp to hunt and scout the path ahead. It was at the end of one day, close to darkness, when they returned carrying Gerik. He was badly hurt and in great pain from a fall that had shattered his leg. A bone was sticking out and I knew his leg would soon become infected. That death was not far away.

At first, he was angry, Furious. I would leave food and tea close to where he could reach so that I could keep my distance and dodge his fists. Trying to block out his screams and curses. Then he became weak, feverish. Sleeping most of the time. His infected leg stank. And his breath. I knew he would be left behind when we returned to the path and I was afraid. Afraid of what would happen to me. That I would be given to another man. Or many men. But I did nothing. I was more afraid of escape.

Then one morning, I awoke early to find the day filled with sun. The sky bright blue, nearly cloudless. The nearby woodlands filled with flowers in bloom. Flowers of every color. Red, yellow, orange like the sunset. Others with colors I had never seen and names I did not know. I left the camp to begin gathering. Breathing in the air's floral scent and feeling strangely light-hearted. I was grateful to be away from the camp. And Gerik.

I ventured further into the woodlands, filling my sack with the different plant leaves that would bring flavor to soups and stews. Seeking the yellow grasses to grind and make into flatcakes. Then, I came upon a small stream and stopped to splash water on my face and arms, delighted to feel clean. I had never traveled this far from the camp, but I was not concerned. I knew the way back. Signs like an old tree or a leaning bush would take me there. Suddenly, I became very tired. I lay on the ground at the edge of a clearing, the grass warm against my body. And fell asleep.

I awakened to hear voices. Soft voices. I thought it was some women from the camp and went to look. There were two horses. Horses much larger than the ones the Zsuirai men rode. Hiding myself behind a large tree, I saw two women. Not Zsuirai women.

I had never before seen anyone like the two women in the clearing. One was tall. Slim. Really only a girl. Her hair golden. Like her honey-colored skin. The other woman was older, shorter. Heavy with a broad nose and black hair tied at the back of her neck. I had never seen hair so black. Or so thick. Nor anyone with honey-colored skin. Or tunics decorated with beads of different shapes and colors. Large beads that, I learned later, were shells. Shells from the sea. Or skirts sewn up on the side of each leg.

I watched as they took off their clothes, threw a cloak on the ground and lay down —the slim honey-colored girl on top of the black-hair woman. Laughing. Kissing. Their hips moving in such a way that they soon began to moan, making sounds of pleasure that filled the air. My mother had told me of women that went off together, especially during the *Synkalos*, the Great Gatherings of the different tribes. But I had never seen two women embracing. Like the two lying on the ground.

I stood behind the tree unable to move. Trembling. But it seemed wrong to watch. I picked up my sack and turned to leave. It was then I saw him. Vjorj. One of the Zsuirai men. A man who, I had heard, was so brutal that the other men feared him. Scowling, he gestured that I stay quiet. That I leave. But I stayed. And watched. Watched as he went over to the women. Watched as he pulled the woman on top off by her hair, punched her, and flung her towards a nearby tree. He turned the other woman on her stomach, held her head up by her hair, and slashed his knife across her throat. Then he mounted her. Suddenly, my mother's face appeared before my eyes.

It was as if I were asleep and had entered a dream. A dream in which I watched myself as I put my sack on the ground, picked up a large branch and, with all my strength, brought it down on Vjorj's head. I watched myself pull him off the woman. But she was dead, her throat cut. Vjorj had entered a dead woman. Now, he too was dead.

I went over to the girl lying by the tree. There was blood everywhere. Her hair. Her face. I was afraid that she too was dead, but then I saw her chest move with breath and she opened her eyes. Large eyes, golden brown in color. Almost the same color as her skin, her hair. She was *chryse*, golden. Beautiful, I thought.

I stopped the bleeding with leaves from my sack and wiped the blood from her face. I saw her trying to cover herself and left to bring her clothes. When I returned, she tried to speak, but I did not know her language.

She was wailing, "Nuun. Nuun."

She saw the other woman was dead. She wept for a time and then gestured that I help her up. I helped her to her feet and then to dress. Helped her to walk over to one of the horses and to mount. She could not sit upright, but clasped her arms around the horse's neck and rode off. Golden hair, blood streaked.

I walked over to the dead woman and covered her with the cloak they had placed on the ground. I left Vjorj uncovered. And still, as if dreaming, I picked up my sack and then a tree branch, making a trail as I made my way back. Dragging my feet along the ground. Slashing back and forth at the underbrush with the branch. Stopping only when I could see the camp in the distance.

Gerik was asleep and I was no longer in the dream. I did not know if I, or Vjorj were missed. I kept myself busy with sorting out the herbs in my sack and cooking a soup to eat. And I waited. Waited until nightfall and then daybreak. Just before the sun rose, I took my sack and blanket, strapped them on my back, and left the camp to hide at the edge of the woodlands. But no one came.

Gerik slept as I waited throughout the next day and night. I never knew a day or night could be so long. When daylight came, I, once again, strapped my sack and blanket on my back and hid in the woodlands. This time I did not have long to wait.

There were perhaps thirty. Shouting their own war cry. Fewer than the Zsuirai men. Some were on horseback. Others on foot, running into the camp with spears and axes. Faces streaked with black paint. Most had honey-colored skin and thick black hair. Like the woman Vjorj had killed. I was filled with fear. Thinking what would happen if the Zsuirai won the battle. But the screams and cries were those of the Zsuirai. This time, the blood on the axes and spears was Zsuirai blood. It did not take long.

As they began to leave the camp, I stepped out of the woodlands and was quickly surrounded by those on horseback. Women? Men? I could not tell. I picked up a tree branch, swinging it along the underbrush and pointing to myself to show them it was I who had made the path to the Zsuirai camp. They talked softly to one another and then one woman — at least, I thought it was a woman — gestured that I mount her horse and sit behind her. I had never ridden a horse before, but one of the other riders dismounted, hiked my skirt up between my legs, and helped me up.

As we rode off, I clasped my arms around her waist. The smell of blood on her clothes. She was a woman. No, a girl. I heard the sound of weeping and wondered who was still alive. If Gerik was still alive. If only the men had been killed. If the Zsuirai were now a tribe of women. I was filled with fear. Afraid that I would fall off the horse. Afraid they would make me a *dolo*. Asking myself, "What have I done?"

It took me a while to match the up and down rhythm of the horse as we followed the others. We rode for a time until we came upon a river and, as I dismounted, I saw the lifeless bodies of two women. Both had been killed in the battle with the Zsuirai. I could now tell the women from the men and saw there were many more women. All were weeping. Wailing. They took off their bloodied clothes, undressed the dead women — and wading into the river, washed their bodies, then themselves and their weapons. The water ran pink. When it was once again clear, they raised their arms and began to chant. I did not know the words, but there was no mistaking the sound of lamentation.

I had never seen so many naked women. It was only the Zsuirai men who saw women without clothes. I watched as they dressed themselves in clean tunics and skirts sewn up the side of each leg. Then, before leaving, they made a fire and burned the bloodied clothes they had worn. Burying the ashes, still chanting. They lifted the two dead women on horses and my rider mounted her horse, gesturing that I should sit behind her. But, once again, I needed help to mount. It took a long time before I was able to leap on a horse.

We separated into small groups, each riding off in a different direction. Throwing branches and underbrush behind to confuse the Zsuirai—if any were still alive to follow. It was a long, hard journey. Riding on trails that led us upward into the mountains, dismounting to lead the horses along narrow rocky paths. When I looked up to the top of the mountain, I saw three trees standing side by side. Tall trees. But then, as we came closer, I saw they were not trees, but women. Three women. Tall women.

When we reached the top, we walked the horses down the mountainside and then through woodlands. It was nearly nightfall when we reached level ground and I saw their camp. On one side were mountains. On the other, water. The great water Tani had described to my mother. Endless as far as I could see.

I had kept my promise. I had left the Zsuirai. I had escaped. Tears came to my eyes as I stood there, unable to move. Watching wave upon wave splashing gently as they reached the shore. But there were no lands that I could see floating on it.

THE ATAI

Where there are mountains, people are not easily subdued

Everything was strange. My mother had lived with three different tribes. I knew only the ways of the Zsuirai. Their camps were for sleeping. For hunting and gathering food before returning to the path. These people were called the Atai and their camp was a place to stay. But it was not a camp. It was a *koru*. A village in a clearing. Home. The first I had ever seen. I learned later that there were other *koru*, both north and south. But this was the largest. Another small camp, not a *koru*, was close to the path so their people could watch the tribes traveling south. Other villages were further south. But they were not Atai.

Surrounding the *koru* was a low wall built of stones, one placed on top of the other. Inside were *domos*. Huts. Large huts. One much larger than the others. All built of blocks of dried mud. Not like the Zsuirai huts that were made from animal skins and underbrush. Nearby, was a circle of flat stones with strips of wood placed on top. For sitting. This was where they gathered for talk and to make their ceremonies. A large stone, engraved with the likeness of a woman, stood at its entrance. A woman with the face of a bird. Their *Diwa*. The Goddess, *Elithe*.

I wondered what kind of people they were. My mother had told me that her tribe, the Naorjai, were a joyous people. Not always on the path, but whenever they made a camp and stayed for a time. The Aziri were a sad people and the Zsuirai, a cruel and angry people. At first, I thought the Atai were a silent people. Then, I understood it was because they were mourning.

There were perhaps forty in all and they held themselves tall. Like my mother. The women as tall as the men. Not like the Zsuirai women who were small. Most had thick black hair that curled down to their shoulders in tangled ringlets, wound in a knot and pinned to the top of their head, or tied at the back of their neck. Many were dark honey in color while others were a golden honey. I began to think of them as the honey people although some had skin almost as light as mine. And I wondered what they thought of me. My pale skin and yellow hair.

I did not see any *Agetes*. Leaders. But there was one woman. An old woman they called Veri, who as far as I could tell, they listened to the most. There were many more women than men and the children were mostly girls. Just a few men and I saw only four young boys. I looked for the girl with the honey-color hair, but she was nowhere to be seen.

Then, one woman gave me a bowl filled with soup. I was about to drink when I saw something I had never seen before. A tiny bowl attached to a stick that they called a *leji*. A spoon. After I had finished eating, my rider gestured that I go into a nearby hut and sleep. I curled up on blankets, much softer than the ones I was used to, and slept.

I woke at sunrise to the sound of chanting and left the hut to see a line of people walking into the woodlands. One woman motioned that I follow as they carried the two dead women and Nuun, the woman Vjorj had killed, to another clearing outside the village. The *koru*. There, inside a circle made of tall sticks tied together so animals could not reach them, the dead women were placed side-by-side on wooden platforms. They chanted for a time and then we returned to the village. Birds circling about the women's bodies.

I learned the Atai left their dead in clearings for birds to feast on. Then, when stripped of all flesh, their bones were taken to woodlands close to the village and buried. Small stones, marked with a *V*, placed on the soil above. It took time to understand they believed that the birds, once having devoured the flesh of the dead, would send their spirits to Earth. To call out to those who came after. What that meant, I did not know.

Once back at the village, I saw her. The golden-hair girl. Weeping. She walked over, touched my shoulder, and my legs weakened. I pointed to myself and said my name, but she did not respond. Just walked away. I would not see her again until after the next full moon.

The Atai talked quietly among themselves, but I was mostly ignored. Left to myself until their mourning time was over. I had many questions. I wanted to know if this was the *Ilios*, the Sunlands. And if so, where were the lands floating on the water? Why were there so few men? Only ten, no more. And why were the young children running about nearly all girls? I wanted to know if their Goddess was a bird, what calling out meant, and who were those that came after. But I had to wait until I knew their language well enough to ask these questions. And to understand their answers.

I spent the days wandering about the village and the nearby woodlands. I would have liked to go down to the sea, but I was afraid. Then, when their mourning time was over, they began to speak. I pointed to myself and said my name. And that I was Naorji. At first, they called me Naorji. But then they understood my name was Ayala and each one, in turn, told me their name. Too many to remember.

The village, their *koru*, became filled with sound. Talking, arguing, humming, singing, laughing, clapping hands. Not like the Zsuiri camp of silent women and quarreling men. They were a touching people. An affectionate people. I tried not to stiffen when one, or another, would touch me. Or, when the children would try to hug me or run their fingers through my hair. I did not want to displease or insult, but I did not like people's hands on me. It was only my mother who had touched me with affection.

The woman I called my rider was Eyann. She was tall, slim. Her nose wide, lips full—chiseled, as if they were carved upon her face. Eyes, the darkest brown, almost black. And skin, a darker

honey color than most of the other Atai. Her hair was black, thick.
Tied at the back of her neck. But, when untied, became a black mist
framing her face.

It was she who showed me where the horses were kept. And
took me down a path that led to the sea, pointing out shells with
tiny bits of food inside. There, near the shore, I saw what they
called *volos*. Boats floating on water that Tani, the Aziri woman, had
described to my mother. And gesturing across the sea, Eyann took
out a small stone she kept in her pouch. A stone engraved with a
picture of two Goddesses. Two Goddesses sitting side by side.

The land surrounding their *koru*, their village, was beautiful.
The changing colors of the sea. Sometimes the same color as the sky.
The green of the woodlands, the flower-filled fields, the graceful
trees that gave shade from the sun. And the nearby hillsides that rose
out of Earth, sloping upwards until they became mountains. Some
with rounded tops—like a woman's breasts. White clouds above.

When I was with the Zsuirai, there was never time to take in
the beauty of the land as we followed the path. Or when we made
camp. The exhaustion of travel. Hunting, trapping, gathering, sewing, cooking—filled the days until nightfall. And then sleep. Here,
there was work, but there was also time. Time to walk the hillside
trails and follow the mountain paths above the village. Time to go
to the sea and walk in the water at the edge of the shore. To lie on
warm sand and look at the clouds move about in the sky. And time
before sleep to watch the stars.

But the beauty of the place was more than the sea and the
mountains that changed color and shape as sunlight, or the darkness
of nightfall, visited them. And the flowers that slipped out of Earth
as the warming time began. All that the Atai made was beautiful.
Their *domo*s, their huts. Water jugs, cooking pots, *volos*. All decorated
with a *V*, or animal heads with horns like the crescent moon. Or with
drawings of birds and flowers. Their spears, bows, arrows, axes. All
painted with different designs and in different colors. Red, yellow,
blue. And their bodies. Red dots on their arms and legs. Strange
markings on their foreheads. Something like a star.

The women and the men wore beads woven throughout their
hair and necklaces made of shells or feathers. Their boots trimmed

with strips of fur and tunics sewn from animal skins pounded thin. Smooth to the touch and decorated with beads and shells of different colors. Nothing like the coarse clothing the Zsuirai wore. Even the horses had beads wound throughout their manes and tails. And now, I too wore a tunic with many beads and a skirt sewn up on the side of each leg they called a *kandagais*. Trousers for riding.

I wanted to be useful and began to gather nuts and fruits, set traps to catch small animals, pound animal skins, and add herbs to their stews. I found the grasses growing in the nearby woodlands that I could make into flatcakes. But when I returned to the village with bunches in my arms, I heard laughter and Eyann showed me yet another circle. One, just outside the village, protected by sticks tied together they called a *circa*. A fence. Grasses growing inside. Planted in Earth. And other plants as well. Some that made *fasi*. Beans. It was then I learned it was not always necessary to go to the woodlands for food.

Food was abundant. Meat from animals that we trapped or hunted. Fish from nearby streams and the sea. Beans, nuts, berries, fruits, grain for flatcakes. And the tiny pieces of meat inside the shells at the edge of the sea. And even more meat in larger shells. When I was with the Zsuirai, there was never enough to eat and I, like the other Zsuirai women, was always hungry. Now I had to learn when to stop eating. To know when I no longer had hunger.

It took me time not to be afraid. I had frightening dreams that filled me with dread. Dreams of Gerik coming for me. That the Zsuirai men would find me and take me back. Dreams that I was on the path alone. I would wake up crying, struggling to find breath. But after a time, the dreams visited less often. And then they stopped.

It was Eyann who taught me to wave my arms and legs and glide through the water. And how to move a *volos* on top of the sea. Who showed me how to make arrows and a bow. And how to shoot. Who told me the golden-hair girl's name was Nahomey and that she was Erati. I did not know what Erati meant. I thought it was another tribe. But I did not have the words to ask.

It took me one, perhaps two cold times, to learn to speak their language. Eyann and the older children helped. Teaching me different words. Pointing out the cooking pots, the different herbs, their tools and weapons. Saying what they were called. Giving me the names of what they did. Cooking, gathering, hunting. Many words ended with a strange sound that was difficult for me to imitate and I could never really speak as they spoke. Some of the Atai would laugh and make jokes when they heard me talk. But I did not mind. I liked their laughter.

Eyann was my first friend. It did not take long to learn she loved to tease. Once, before I knew their language well enough to speak, I pointed to a *V* painted on a hut and waved a finger at a bird flying above. And then to two crescent-shaped axes bound together and gestured towards the sky. Eyann nodded. Then, moved her hand down to rest between her legs. The place where a child entered Earth. The place of pleasure. I could feel my face flush, become hot. Hearing her laughter.

I soon became friends with two other women. Suaja and Liki. And Nooga, Suaja's brother. At first, when Nooga came near me, I would become frightened and draw away. Thoughts of Gerik and the other Zsuirai men made these feelings inside of me. But, as my memories of the Zsuirai began to fade, I saw that he was as gentle as many of the Atai women. Even more so. It was he who showed me how to place the tiny seeds in moistened Earth. Speaking words of gratitude to *Elithe* for the grain that would soon appear.

Before darkness came, the Atai would practice spear-throwing, hurling axes, and shooting arrows while riding horses. The woman and the men. To see who were the most skilled. To know who was prepared to fight. There were many contests. Competitions. Running, wrestling. Who was the fastest? The strongest? I had never witnessed such fierce determination to excel and watched, astonished. The women I had known, the Zsuirai women, were forbidden to use weapons and although my mother had taught me how to make a spear, I never thought women could be warriors.

At nightfall, we would make fires and all of us would gather in the stone circle. To sing, play games, dance. To say what had happened during the day. What plants had been gathered, which animals trapped, how many fish caught. The dreams that had visited the night before, and to share stories about those who no longer lived, and others passed down by those long gone. To lament the dead.

Sometimes there were talks to make peace between those who quarreled. There were many disagreements. Accusations tossed back and forth. Yelling. Cursing. Insulting one another. And twice, I saw two women fight so fiercely that they had to be separated by force. Their disagreements were mostly about who was best at spear throwing or shooting arrows while on horseback, who had won a race, or was doing less than their share of planting and setting traps. Or wanting the same woman. But Eyann told me that some were pretend arguments. Accusations said in fun.

At first, when voices were loud, I became frightened. Until Eyann said, "Ayala. You do not have to be afraid. You are here. Not there."

I understood. They were the Atai. Not the Zsuirai.

Almost every night, they danced. Not like the Zsuirai men. Stamping and jumping. The Atai danced in circles. Sometimes alone. At times, with another person. I would join them in song, but I would not dance. I was clumsy. Stiff. Afraid that they would mock me. But Eyann told me I should not think about how I looked, but let the music move my body to the sounds of reed pipes and *pani*. Drums made from animal skins pounded thin and stretched tight over small gourds. To take the sound of the *pani* into my body and make the music and my body one. It took time to stop thinking about how I looked. And then I began to dance. But never like the Atai. Their grace and ease. And playfulness.

They made many ceremonies. Ceremonies that praised and gave gratitude to *Elithe*. One ceremony was held at the beginning of the warming time, the planting time when Earth welcomed seed. It was then I saw Nahomey dance. She was a *Banta*. Dancer. I had never before seen anyone dance like Nahomey. She began dancing alone. Then, with another *Banta*. Their bodies oiled. Serpentine, snake-like. Coiling about each other. Nahomey's leg between the other woman's legs as their hips circled. Liquid. Melting, one into the other as if they were one. I could feel the wetness between my legs.

It was later that Eyann explained the dance. It was to make desire. Desire to love-make with a woman. To take a man inside so that a child would be birthed. Desire so Earth—moist with dew—would open to seed.

Other ceremonies were held during both the warm and the cool times when food rose out of Earth. Always in *Safretesi*. Sacred places. One in a hillside cave that took us deep in Earth. A second in a grove surrounded by the tallest trees I had even seen. Another was held near the top of a mountain close to the sky. And still another took place along the shore where two sparkling streams of waters—*Safreti*, sacred waters—flowed towards each other. Like two narrow rivers, separated by a strip of sand, meeting in the blue-green sea. It was the Atai's most sacred place. To me, it was wondrous.

There was another ceremony, a strange ceremony when the Atai made lamentations for grieving mothers. Mothers who birthed babies who had died and were called *Olejs*. Something I did not understand until I spoke their language well enough to ask Eyann to explain. But even then, I saw she was hesitant and did not want to talk.

It took time for me to feel desire. Time to forget Gerik and how he would plunge into me. And Vjorj who entered Nuun after he had killed her. I knew which Atai women went only with women. And those who went with both women and men. I could see how some women looked at me. How Eyann looked at me. I never knew I would want a woman—but when desire came, it was the golden-hair woman, Nahomey, I wanted.

Nahomey had no interest in me. Ignored me. When I asked Eyann why, she replied she did not know, but said perhaps it was because I reminded her of what had happened in the clearing. What the man had done to Nuun.

I knew that Eyann went with different women. And sometimes, men. I wanted to know how she could love more than one person at the same time. What she would feel if the person she loved went with another.

She seemed surprised by my questions and thought for a while before speaking. "Sometimes I am angry that she is not with me. Sometimes I am sad."

"You are not *esilai*? Jealous?"

She did not understand the word and asked, "What is that? What is *esilai*?"

"Resentment. Wanting something that someone else has. You are not afraid that she will love another more? Leave you for another? Not return?"

"Sometimes. Not always. But I am also happy that she is happy."

"You are happy?"

"Yes. It is not always love. Sometimes it is just desire. The excitement you feel when you love-make with a new *amayo*. A different person."

"Women do fight over a woman."

"Yes, but we think that is *katilos*. Inappropriate."

There was much for me to learn.

Then I asked, "The women. Some go with men?"

"Yes. When they want to make a child. Many go with both women and men."

"Who are the men to make a child with? The Atai men? There are so few."

"Sometimes. But more with the men at the Great Gatherings where many tribes meet. It is there we make children."

I saw the Atai were a laughing people, a joyous people. Singing, dancing, joking, teasing. But there was worry beneath their laughter. Fear. Fear of the tribes traveling south. Not those they called the *Nonopati*. People struggling to stay alive and reach the *Ilios*, the Sunlands. But the others. The *Areia*. Tribes my mother had called the *Tardos*. War tribes like the Zsuirai. Afraid they would find their villages. That there would be too many of them to fight and they would have to flee. To the mountains. To another land. Leave their *koru*. Their home.

I knew they had many questions. Why had I led them to the Zsuirai. Why had I betrayed my tribe. But the Zsuirai were not my tribe. I could have followed Nahomey to their village. Or waited in the clearing for someone to come for Nuun. Or escaped further into the woodlands. To where, I did not know. But I knew that if I did not return to the camp, the Zsuirai would search for me. And Vjori. And perhaps find the Atai villages.

I had seen what they did to people who they found on the path. Or in the woodlands. And to those who tried to escape. Yes, I made a trail to the Zsuirai camp for the Atai to find. But it was as if I were dreaming. Not acting out of thought — or with a plan in mind. It did not matter. Dreaming, or thinking, I would have done the same.

EYANN

How could she could breathe through such a nose?

I t was the faint whinny of a horse that told us they were near. We were waiting to tease them. Suaja, Liki and I. But it was Nahomey who appeared. Alone. Clinging to her horse and barely conscious. Her face bruised, her hair streaked with blood. Nuun was nowhere to be seen. We helped her to dismount, but she could barely speak and it took her time to say what had happened. That a man had killed Nuun. That a strange woman had killed the man.

We knew the place. We brought Nahomey back to the village and mounted our horses. As we entered the clearing, we saw Nuun and a man lying on the ground. Both dead. Nuun's throat had been cut and there was blood between her legs. The man's head was crushed. He was broad in the shoulders with yellowish hair scattered all over his body. Chest, arms, legs. Like the war people. The *Areia*.

We lifted Nuun's body onto her horse and were about to return to our village, leaving the man for the birds and animals to eat, when Liki saw slashed underbrush and markings on the ground. It was a trail that led away from the clearing. A trail that the woman Nahomey spoke of must have made. Why she had made a trail for us to see, we did not know. Why she had killed the man and who

she was, we did not know. We wondered if she was one of them.
The war people on the path.

Suaja brought Nuun back to the village while Liki and I
mounted our horses and followed the trail. Riding until we saw
a camp in the distance. We tied our horses to a tree and crawled
towards the camp, concealing ourselves at the edge of the woodlands. Close by were a few men. But we saw no women. The men
looked like the dead man. Broad in the shoulders. Clumps of yellow
hair on their bodies.

Liki and I spoke quietly. Wondering if the man who had killed
Nuun was of this tribe, this camp. Convinced they were the *Areia*.
Why the unknown woman had led us here, we did not know. But
we knew what we had to do. If they were the *Areia*, we could not let
them continue along the path. It would mean a battle. It would not
be the first. Nor the last.

Liki rode back to the village to gather our people while I hid
in the woodlands. Waiting, shivering as nightfall came, then day.
Then another night. It was nearly daybreak when she and the others returned. The camp was quiet. The people asleep. Some of us
rode horses while others ran into the camp—swinging axes, hurling spears, shooting arrows. There were many more of them than
us, but they were unprepared. When it was over, all of the men
were dead, or dying. And two of our people, two women, had been
killed. We did not kill the women, or the children, but left them in
the camp. Shrieking, weeping as we made ready to ride to a nearby
river. Whoever they were, they were now a tribe of women. Too
many for us to take.

It was then I saw her. Standing at the edge of the woodlands near
the camp. Sweeping a tree branch along the ground to show us she
was the one who had made the trail for us to follow. I spoke briefly
to the others and then gestured that she mount and sit behind me on
my horse. But she did not know how. Liki raised the woman's skirt
between her legs and helped her up. We rode off to the river—all
in different directions— away from the trail the woman had made.
We did not want to leave any signs that could lead to our village.

The woman clasped her arms around my waist, but it took her
time to learn the rhythm of my horse. I had never seen anyone who

looked quite like her. Tangled yellow hair. Her mouth small, her nose thin. I wondered how she could breathe through such a nose. And pale. Skin pink, almost white. Eyes, a color I had never seen before. Blue. Light blue. Her face showed such a sadness that I wondered what had been done to her. And she was thin. Terribly thin. Later, when she had learned our language, I asked her why she was so thin when she first came to us.

She said, "The men eat first."

I had never heard of such a thing.

When we reached the river, we dismounted, undressed and, wading into the water, washed the two dead women and ourselves. Chanting lamentations. We set fire to our bloodied clothes, then buried the ashes, dressed ourselves in the clean garments we had brought — and mounted our horses to return to our village. The woman sitting behind me. Once again, we rode in different directions, concealing our trail with underbrush and branches. Still fearful that we could be followed. It was a long journey and there was much to do. Much to discuss. To make lamentations. To leave three dead women outside our village. And we had a strange woman with us. Perhaps she was one of the *Areia*. The woman who had led us to their camp.

It was a sadness time. A silent, mourning time until the bones of the three women were brought back and buried in the nearby woodlands. We did not know what the strange woman understood, but she seemed to accept our silence. We had never before brought a stranger to our village. A woman who did not know our language, or how to ride a horse. One who did not know what to do with a *leji*, a spoon. Or what a *volo*, a boat was. A woman who went into the woodlands to gather grasses and plants that grew near our village. But then she said her name. Ayala. It was the way she said it. Her voice. Her strange blue eyes. I began to like her.

She quickly joined in to help. Gathering, trapping, pounding animal skins, cooking. She was as good as our best gatherers and trappers. As skilled as our best healers. But it was her cooking that was a gift. She made food delicious. Spreading animal fat and herbs on roasting meats. Flavoring flatcakes with nuts and juices from berries. I had never tasted meat so tender. Nor cakes so sweet.

She learned quickly. First, a few words, then more words. It was not long before she was able to understand and speak our language. Perhaps two cold times. Although there were sounds she could not make and words she could not speak. She had many questions. Who was my birth mother? What is an Erati? Why are there so few men? So few boy children? Who are the goddesses joined together and why is our Goddess, *Elithe*, a bird? I thought very carefully how I should answer what she asked. And I had many questions as well.

I saw that she was kind. Determined. Determined to learn to mount and ride a horse. Determined to wave her arms and move through the water. To shoot arrows, throw spears, hurl axes. But it took time for her to lose her fear of men and not be frightened when there were quarrels between us. Time for the evil dreams to stop visiting as she slept and her face to lose its sadness. And even more time to laugh.

I wondered what had happened to her. What her life had been like before she came to us. Then my liking turned to wanting. I had always liked to be with more than one lover, one *amayo*. More than one woman, or one man. But now, I could think only of her. Her slim body. Her eyes. Her way of speaking. But I saw that she wanted Nahomey. I knew I had to wait. How long, I did not know. Nahomey was beautiful. I was not.

It was I who told Ayala that Nahomey was Erati. But she did not know what an Erati was. I did not warn her. Say she should not love Nahomey. That it would end in hurt. Nahomey was always with more than one woman. Or, one man. But she wanted each one to be only with her. Nahomey loved only to be admired. Yet, she had loved Nuun.

When she had learned our language, she began to speak about her life. Her mother, Yanija. Her tribe, the Naorji. Her blood kin who she called her *Eshar*. And the stories her mother had told to her. Stories that were passed down about the cold and ice that had reached the steppes of their northern homelands, making Earth dust. That hunger and the many deaths had led her people to travel a path south, believing it would take them to a place they called the *Ilios*, the Sunlands.

It was then I asked, "What is it you call the *Ilios*?"

"It is a land on the shore of a great sea with large lands floating upon it."

"Our sea has lands floating upon it, but they are too far out to see."

She stopped for a while, then said, "Perhaps this is the *Ilios*, the Sunlands. Your *volos*, your boats. Can they take you to them?"

"Sometimes. Not often."

It was now nightfall. Time to rest. Days passed and then she began again. Telling me about her mother and how her voice had been taken by a man from a war tribe that had attacked her people. Slashed her throat so she could no longer speak, only whisper. And how her mother had been found by another tribe, the Aziri, and befriended by a woman called Tani.

She said, "It was when we were with the Aziri that I was birthed. Then the Zsuirai came. And took us. My mother and I."

Then I asked her what I had long wanted to understand. "Why did you kill the man? You lived with his tribe. Why did you lead us to their camp?"

"They were not my tribe. Yes, I killed the man. Yes, I made a trail to lead your people to their camp. But I am Naorji, not Zsuirai. I saw what happened. I knew the man who attacked Nahomey. Who killed Nuun. Who entered her after he had killed her. He was *badjo*. An evil. Like many of the Zsuirai men. I can only say it was like I was dreaming. I killed as if I were in a dream. And in the same dream, perhaps it was a spell, I made the trail and waited. I believed your people would come and help me escape the Zsuirai. I did not think much beyond that."

"This is what you thought? What you wanted?"

"Yes. It was my mother who first spoke of escape. It was she who told me to go to a people in the woodlands. I did not want to live with the Zsuirai. But I was afraid and so I waited. The Zsuirai were a war tribe. They killed. The men would fight one another and sometimes one would kill another. They lived to attack other tribes. To kill and to take. And leave those who were ill or injured. On the path to die."

"To die?"

"Yes. To die on the path. I saw such cruelty. Towards each other. Towards the women. They made women *dolos*. Slaves. Beating them."

"The women did not fight back?"

"The men were big. The women small."

"The men were bigger than the women?"

"Yes. Taller."

"Taller? Why?"

"Perhaps because the men took the food. Even the boy children were given more food than girl children."

"Perhaps the men chose small women to mate with."

She did not understand.

I said, "You are not small."

"I am Naorji."

"Do Zsuirai women go with both women and men?"

"No. Forbidden. But my mother did tell me of some women that went with women. Saying it had to be a secret, or they would be punished. Left on the path. I did see men taking young boys to the woodlands. And enter them, willing or not."

Then she asked, "You go with both women and men?"

"Yes. With men it is a different pleasure."

"I had no pleasure with Gerik."

"No pleasure?"

"No. Mostly pain when he entered me."

"Entered? To us it is not entering. No one enters me. When I want, I take a man inside of me. I move him inside me. I move him how I want. You did not want other men?"

"No. What pleasure would there be?"

This was our most intimate conversation.

Then I asked, "Did you have children?"

"One. She did not live."

"You did not want another?"

"No. I could not escape with a child."

I had two more questions. I asked her what the Zsuirai Goddess was called.

"He is called, *Hjis*."

"He?"

"Yes, he."

This was what surprised me the most. A man goddess. We were quiet for a time and then I asked, "Did Gerik beat you?"

"Only at the end."

"Why did you not leave him?"

"I was given to Gerik so that I would not be given to other men. If you do not belong to a man, other men can take you. Enter you as they please. I belonged to Gerik. Owned. If I birthed children, they would be his. Because it would be only he who made children with me."

It was difficult to understand what she was saying. What *owned* or *given* meant. *Taken* by other men. And that children belonged to the men. That a man would care if he was not the one who made a child with a woman. Why would he care when the daughters of his mother, his sisters, birthed children?

And then Ayala wept. Wept for a long time. And I held her in my arms. Light skin against dark.

PART TWO ⚜ CHAPTER 6

AYALA

Love shook my heart
Like a fierce wind
Troubling the oaks on a high mountain.

— Sappho, 6th century BCE

We were lying at the edge of the woodlands, the grass warm against our bodies. I saw Eyann looking at me and I suddenly felt such a wanting, a desire so intense that I had never felt before. I turned towards her, stroking her face. She drew me closer. Our lips touched. First gently, then hard as her tongue entered my mouth.

For a moment I thought of Gerik jamming himself into me. And Vjorj. But there was only Eyann. Her softness and the wetness moving down my legs as we unfastened our tunics and pulled down our trousers. Lying naked against each other. Hands, mouth, tongues exploring. I never before had someone's mouth between my legs. A trembling, melting warmth spread throughout my body. My heart, my body pounding. Shaking, shuddering. I heard myself, as if at a distance, cry out. Then, Eyann's cry. And we held each other close and slept.

We were what my mother had called *erojai*. Lovers. Who the Atai called *amayos*. Everyone teased us. Clapping hands, applauding us as we walked by. Making kissing sounds. Liki said she had been waiting. Suaja told me how happy she was. We were now *hyati*, new *amayos*. Inseparable. Love-making as often as we could. Gathering, hunting, catching fish—always together. Indulged at first but then, as time passed, we were expected to be apart. Otherwise, Eyann said we would be *katilos*. Inappropriate. That is what she told me.

But the nights were ours. And sometimes the days when we would ride our horses along the shore, or up the hillsides to the mountains to see the beauty of the land and sea from a distance. Lying on warm rocks to watch the sky.

I had loved two people. My mother. And my infant daughter, but only for a few days. Eyann was my first *amayo* and I had never loved with such abandon as I loved her. Loved Eyann. I did have fear she would go with another. Have another *amayo*. Or tire of me. But I said nothing. I knew what she would say. That she was here now.

I thought I knew what I looked like. I had seen my face in rivers and streams. But Eyann brought over a small round stone that showed my face clearly. I did not like what I saw. Pale skin, thin lips, small nose. Eyann said not to look at just my nose or lips, but my face. And I began to like what I saw. My face was no longer marked by sorrow. Happiness filled my face. I was the happiest I had ever been. I could swing axes, glide through water, steer a *volos*, ride horses—although I could not ride and shoot arrows at the same time. I was with Eyann. I was no longer Naorji. I was Atai.

It was the beginning of the cool time and the leaves were turning yellow when Eyann told me a Great Gathering was to be held. She called it something that I could not speak, but I knew it was what my mother had described. A *Synkalos*. There was much excitement. Much to prepare before we began the long journey. Decorating tunics. Making jewelry, spears, bows and arrows to trade. Gathering fruits and nuts and cooking flatcakes to eat along the way.

We rode our horses south, first up the hillsides and then the mountains, joined by those from the Atai villages both north and south. Stopping at nightfall, wrapped in warm cloaks and blankets, to sleep beneath the stars. We rode for three nights and then a half day before we heard the sound of *pani*, drums. And people singing. Ahead of us was a large clearing in the woodlands. The air fragrant from stews cooking on fires.

I had never seen so many people at one time. More than the Zsuirai. Many different tribes. Many fires. Women and men. But many more women. Faces painted, arms and legs decorated with dots of different colors. My eyes could not take in all there was to see

I wanted to stay close to Eyann, but she had disappeared. When I asked Liki where she went, she told me she had gone off to see a woman. One who had once been an *amayo*. A sharp sadness entered me. *Esilai*, jealousy. All I could do was pretend to be unconcerned. To appear happy. But Eyann soon returned. Hugging me. Kissing me. I did see Nahomey, but she did not look at me.

I was a stranger. A stranger at the Gathering. I saw many people looking at me. My yellow hair and pale skin. Children would try to touch me as they ran by. But then, I saw two women who looked like me and I wanted to know if, they too, had escaped. But when we tried to speak, we could not understand each other. Our talk was too different. Liki told me they did not escape, but had left their tribe on the path. To live with another people they had found in the woodlands. Why, she did not know.

The days were filled with competitions. Contests. Wrestling, spear throwing, shooting arrows while riding horses. Story-telling. And many ceremonies praising *Elithe* and another Goddess, *Cybe*. As nightfall grew near, fires were made and small sticks lit, making smoke to breathe in. Then, sweet juices in pitchers were passed about to drink—bringing on even more laughter. And dancing. Dancing in circles and long lines winding about the clearing. Waving arms. Waving hips. Then the *bantas*. The dancers. Nahomey and others. Some shaking long sticks so the dance seemed more like a battle. Dancing warriors.

When darkness came, many went into the woodlands. Those who stayed behind clapped their hands, making kissing noises, and mimicking women with big bellies. Bellies filled with a child. Eyann and I went along with the others. At first, I was hesitant, but I could

see this was what she wanted. And so we love-made in the woodlands. Our cries of pleasure mingling with those nearby. Echoing
throughout the night.

The Gathering lasted three days and nightfalls. Liki won a
spear-throwing contest and a woman from the Atai village north was
said to be among the best at shooting arrows while riding a horse. I
was happy to return to our *kuru*. Our village. Wondering if any of
the Atai women would birth children.

It was then that I began to ask Eyann questions. What I had
wondered about for so long. I asked if the Atai people had traveled
south on the path, then left to make their village in the woodlands.

Eyann answered, "No. We were not on the path. Some say we
are from here. That we were made here. But there are other stories
passed down from long ago. From the time of the *Achios*, the Ancient
ones. Stories that told how we were made in a great land far, far
south. That we came here hundreds of full moons ago, moving our
volos across a large sea. Passing by many lands. Stopping at others.
Until we reached here."

"You came from the south?"

"Yes."

"Why did you stop here?"

"The stories said we were to make a village, a *koru*, on a hillside that became a mountain. Close to a sea where two streams of
waters would meet. *Safretesi* waters. Two streams flowing side-by-
side. Where we make our ceremonies. And so we are here. Then
other villages were made. Both north and south. We are one great
tribe. Except for those much further south."

Then I asked, "You have who we called *Agetes*? Leaders?"

"No. We have elders. Old ones who are wise. Like Veri. And
others who are skilled in battle. That is all."

"You have fought many battles?"

"No. Not many. There have been battles, but I have fought
only twice. Once, when two women were missing. Two women
from the village north. Taken by the *Areia*. We attacked their camp
and brought the women back. Another time we found some men
scouting close to our village. Men like the ones in the Zsurai camp.
Light hair all over their bodies. We knew if they were missed, others

would be sent to find them. And so we fought. First, we killed the men. Then we attacked their tribe."

I was quiet for a time. Then I asked, "Eyann, who is your mother?"

"You mean the mother who birthed me?"

"Yes."

"Ayala, I am from a strong mother-line. Who you call the *Eshar*. Blood kin. I have many mothers. The mother who birthed me. Her sisters. Their oldest daughters. I drank at many breasts. We know who our birth mothers are. We are special to the women who birth us. But we are cared for by all. From the time I was birthed, I slept in many different huts. In the villages both north and south. We share all. Food, fire, huts, planting fields. And children. Even lovers. *Amayos*."

She looked at me. Smiling.

There was much to understand.

I said, "The two Goddesses. The ones who sit side-by-side. The ones joined together. Who are they?"

"We do not know. They were left by a people who we think live across the sea. Who perhaps were here. But our *volos* do not travel so far. Sister Goddesses. Lover Goddesses. We do not know."

"Your *Diwa*. Your Goddess. She is a bird?"

"No, Ayala. *Elithe* is not a bird. *Elithe* is *Tawa*. Earth. We do not worship birds. *Elithe* has the qualities of a bird. That is why we show Her with a face of a bird. Birds give feathers, food. Round shells with life inside. Eggs. Eggs make life. *Elithe* makes life. *Elithe* nurtures and protects us. Like birds who feed and protect their young in nests high up in trees. Birds are free. They fly throughout the sky. Sometimes so high we can no longer see them. They swim, they sing, dance. They are *Safreti*. Sacred.

"And birds eat the flesh of the dead. Then, those who have died will pass through them. Spilling down, entering Earth. Becoming spirit. Because we are spirit, we do not disappear. We are Earth. We nourish trees and grasses and plants that make food for people. For animals. We make flowers to decorate the land. More than that, our spirit remains in Earth and calls out to those who can hear. To those who will return. To those who come after."

"Call out?"

"Yes. But not with a voice. A presence. A presence that those who come after can sense. Not all, but some will feel sorrow. Grief. Sometimes joy."

"Sorrow? Why?"

"Because they may sense that what has happened here was bad."

"And joy?"

"Because we do not disappear. Our spirit remains in Earth for all time. We are not forgotten. We are those who came before. To tell those who come after that we are—joined. Bound together across time. We are one across time."

"This is what you believe?"

"Yes. This is so."

I was quiet for a time. Then I asked, "Who are the Erati?"

Eyann replied, "There is a mother-line who we call the Erati. Women, some but not all, who birth daughters that have the gift of hearing messages. Prophecy. It is a gift. Sometimes a curse."

"Nahomey. She is Erati. She has this gift?"

"Yes. And another woman. One who lives in the village north. Only two. We call them, *Aimajs*. Messengers."

"They are *hiera*? Priestesses?"

"No. *Aimajs* are messengers who can help us to know the coming times. They receive messages that tell us what can happen. What we need to do."

"How? How does this happen?"

"We choose a question that the *Aimaji* will ask. Then she will prepare to receive the message."

"A message? From whom?"

"We do not know. Our stories do not tell who receives the question. Or who sends the message. Perhaps it is *Elithe*. Perhaps it is the spirits of those who came before. Now in Earth."

I remembered my mother once showed me a plant that brought on dreaming. Visions to tell the coming times. And so, I asked, "How do the *Aimajs* do this? Eat something? A plant from the woodlands?"

"No. Nothing is eaten."

Eyann waited a moment, then said, "A certain kind of snake is chosen. Caught. Brought to the *Aimaji*. A small snake that is allowed to bite her. A gentle bite. Not deep, or it will send too much poison and she will die. It is the bite of the snake that lets the *Aimajs* enter the coming times."

"A snake?"

"Yes. Snakes live in Earth. Near the spirits of those who came before."

It was hard to believe that anyone would let a snake, even a small snake, bite them.

"Eyann, you said a gift and a curse. Why a gift? Why a curse?"

"It is a gift to our people when we need to know the coming times. When we need to know what can happen. To understand what we must do. How we must prepare."

"And a curse?"

"Yes. It is a curse because the *Aimaji* will never be the same. The message will mark her. Change her. If there is horror in the coming times, she will see it. Feel it."

"It is a message?"

"Yes, but not in words. She will see. Hear. Smell. She will feel what will happen. Then, she will tell the message to another woman. One who is chosen. Who we call an *Akrota*. A listener. A woman who will hear what the *Aimaji* says and tell our older ones. Like Veri and others who will understand its meaning. And the *Akrota* will be marked as well. Marked by what she has heard. For both, it can be like an evil dream, a nightmare that will not end with awakening."

"When did this last happen? You have seen this?"

"Yes. Perhaps five cold times ago."

"And the message?"

"Stamping was heard. Feet crushing plants."

"What did it mean?"

"Veri and the other older ones said it could mean the *Areia*. The war people on the path."

"What did you do?"

"We waited. We made weapons. We learned to fight. We became warriors."

Then she said, "No more. It is nightfall."

We lay in each other's arms and slept.

When the sun appeared in the sky, I began again, asking what I was most curious about. Why there were so few men. So few boy children.

Eyann hesitated, then began to speak. "When a boy is birthed, the old ones will come to see the child. To see if he is *Olejs*."

"What is *Olejs*?"

"An *Olejs* is a child who will become what you call *badjo*. An evil when he grows older. A destroyer."

"An evil? An infant?"

"Yes. An infant grows. Becomes a boy, then a man."

"How do the old ones know? How do they decide?"

"Not decide. Watch. See. Hear. Smell. Sense. How the child feeds at a woman's breast. That it is difficult for him to be still. Content. The sounds he makes when he cries. Sometimes his scent. The smell of his *ouro*. Urine. Veri and the other old ones know who are *Olejs*."

"Can they be wrong?"

"No. If they are uncertain, the child, or children, are allowed to live longer. But if they see them hitting, kicking others, taking food from other children. Quick to anger. Then they know. If it is determined that they are *Olejs*—at birth, or later—they cannot live. They grow. They become men. Destroyers. Poisoners of the earth. The *Areia*. It is not in them to see another person as a human. As a person. Or an animal as a living, feeling creature."

"What do you do?"

Again, Eyann hesitated, then she said, "We give the child a drink. One that will bring on sleep. Then, death. They have no pain. This is what we ask of the mothers who birth *Olejs* sons. We know that they suffer. We make lamentations. We mourn with them."

I was silent for a time. Then I asked, "How can you do this?"

"We do this."

"How can you?"

"We do this, but sometimes it is not clear. A child may show signs of what we call, *erith*, aggressiveness, but he is not exactly *olejs*. We watch carefully and reprimand often. But when he becomes man-age and the *erith*, the aggressiveness, continues, we banish him. He must leave us.

"Ayala, the stories passed down from the Ancient ones—the *Achios*—tell us that in the very early times, hundreds of cold times ago, there were many *Olejs*. Men who did much harm. Fighting, hurting others. Entering women by force. Then, an *Aimaji* received a message saying that *Olejs* sons must be put to death. At birth. Or soon after. This was done and, after a time, there were no more *Olejs* men.

"But *Olejs* were still being birthed. And the stories told that some mothers, those who could not bear to have their infant sons killed, ran off. Fled north with their *Olejs* child. There, more and more *Olejs* were born and, after a time, became a people. A brutish people. But we did not know then they would return. Who you call the *Tardos*. Who we call the *Areia*. The war people. War tribes who travel the path south. Who will go far. Who will go everywhere. South, east, west. And do much harm. To people. Animals. Earth. We fear there will come a time when there will be too many to fight and we will have to flee. Then, we will need a message."

"From Nahomey?"

"No. The Erati woman in the village north. Nahomey can no longer be *Aimajs*. Because of what happened in the clearing. More than that, she is like a child. She could not endure a difficult message."

"Eyann, the ancient ones. The *Achios*. Who are they?"

"The first mother-line who made us. The Atai."

I was silent. Then I asked, "If we must flee, where will we go?"

"To the mountains. To the north. The east. Perhaps further."

I thought about how one could kill a small infant. A helpless child. Leaving their mothers in anguish. Wondering how can they do this. Then, I remembered. The Zsuirai. Gerik. And Vjorj.

PART TWO ⚜ CHAPTER 7

THE MESSAGE

I endure it all
For love of you.

— Sappho, 6th century BCE

It was the beginning of the warming time. Three women had birthed children. Two were girls. The third, a boy. Not an *Olejs*. There was much celebration. Clapping hands. Dancing. But the boy did not live past three nightfalls. Although his cries were strong.

Eyann had told me there was much talk at the Gathering about the war tribes. More people, larger tribes than ever had been seen before were on the path. Exploring the woodlands close to the villages north. They were gatherers. Thin, hungry. Searching for nuts, fruits. Anything that could be eaten. But there were others. Many others. Men with weapons. The *Areia*.

Four of us were sent to watch. Myself, Eyann, and two other women. We hid in the woodlands and waited. It did not take long before we saw them. The *Areia* on horseback. Scouting. They looked like the Zsurai. Broad shoulders and clumps of yellow hair on their bodies. I tried to conceal my fear, but seeing them brought back what I did not want to remember. The killing on the path. Vjorj. Gerik. Eta's bruised face. The people I had lived with for most of my life.

We waited until they rode past and then returned to tell the others. All of us filled with fear. Afraid of what might happen if they found our villages. If there was a battle and we were outnumbered. There was much talk and the telling of dreams. One woman told of a frightening dream. A dream of an ancient woman—a skeleton woman—lying on top a pile of other skeleton. Skeletons piled high above Earth.

We met with those who lived in the villages north and south. Some wanted to flee. Others wanted to stay and fight. But we waited and then more of the *Areia* were seen. Some close to our village. It was Eyann who told me. The *Aimaji* who lived north was preparing. Cleansing herself with special herbs. Fasting. An *Akrota*, a listener, had been chosen. A question decided. And a small snake found and brought to the *Aimaji's* breast. She had asked the question. Soon we would know the message.

It was not long before we heard the sound of hoof beats and shouting as two women rode down from the north. The *Akrota* had told the old ones a terrible message. The *Aimaji* had seen gray smoke, Felt Earth crumbling. Watched black waters sweeping over the woodlands. Weeping was heard throughout our village. Wailing. Veri told us we must flee.

I asked Eyann, "Where will we go?"

"Some will ride horses and follow the shoreline north, then cross to the east. To another land."

"The others?"

"To the sea in *volos*. Women about to birth. And the children."

"There are enough *volos*?"

"There will be. Yes."

"Where will they go?"

"To lands floating on the sea. Perhaps to the land of the two Goddesses. To make other *koru*. Other homes."

"And us? You and I?"

"We will ride north. With Liki, Suaja, and Nooga. Veri too. And others."

We prepared to flee. Watching as those in the villages to the south passed and began to make their way north. We built many *volos*. Gathered as much food as possible. Then, we burned all the food that could not be taken. Burned the grasses we had planted in Earth. Burned our *domos*. Our huts. We left nothing but some pots. A few filled with water, others with soup. Poisoned, Eyann told me. The Atai village, once beautiful, was gone. No more. Everything, everyone gone. Liki, Suaja, her brother, Nooga, gone. And Veri. All riding north.

Eyann said, "You must catch up to them. I will stay with a few others. We need to conceal the trails with underbrush. To be certain that the *volos* and those on horses following the shoreline north will not be in their sight. Then we will flee."

"You will follow us?"

"Yes."

"When?"

"Soon. Unless there is a fight."

"A fight?"

"Yes."

"Then I must stay."

"No. You cannot. You have never fought. You have never killed."

"I have killed. I killed Vjork."

"That was not the same."

As Eyann looked at me, she understood I would not leave her. And so, we both stayed. Carrying underbrush and branches to conceal the trails of those riding north and watching the last of the *volos* move out of sight. Then, along with the others who had remained behind, we mounted our horses and prepared to leave. But we had waited too long. There were shouts and the sound of men drawing near. And then the war cry. *Alala*. A cry I had heard before. The Zsuirai.

We dismounted, throwing spears, hurling axes, shooting arrows. There were ten of them. We were six. Eyann was right. I had never killed like this before. But when I saw a man coming towards her, all hesitation left and I brought him down with my spear. Then another. It was quick. When the battle ended, all of the *Areia* were dead. Or dying.

There was no time to bury our bloodied clothes. Eyann and I mounted our horses and began to ride towards the others, following the shoreline north. But then there was shouting and the sound of hoof beats. We were cut off. We had no choice, but to dismount, leave our horses, and turn back. I grabbed my sack and followed Eyann. Running at the edge of the shore on a path that would take us up the hillsides, then the mountains. What happened to the others, we did not know.

As we began to make our way, Eyann whispered, "We need to hide. We cannot follow and lead them to the others riding north. We will go later. On foot. Ride, if we can find our horses. I know a cave. It is not far."

I could see that she was trying to conceal her fear. We moved slowly, trying not to leave a trail. Then, I tripped. Fell. I looked down to see blood on my leg. A small cut. It had begun to rain. First lightly. Then heavy. Soon loud voices told us they were drawing near.

"Here," Eyann said, pointing to an opening on the hillside. "The cave."

We gathered underbrush and dead branches, dragging them behind us as we crawled in. The scent of flowers, a glimpse of gray sky—and we covered the entrance as best we could. Each of us holding our breath as the voices came closer and passed. Then silence.

Eyann whispered, "We will stay for a while. To daybreak. We need not be frightened. We have food. We can stay longer."

I nodded. Nuts and berries were in my sack. But there was little room. The cave was small, just an opening in the hillside. We could not stand. Just sit. Crouch. Nightfall came and we slept for a time, waking to the sound of rain and rocks crashing down the hillside. The cave was now completely dark. Frightened, Eyann and I pushed at the entrance. First with our spears, then with our arms and legs. But it was blocked. A pile of rocks wedged tight against each other. Blocking the opening.

We tried, once more, to push the rocks away. And then again, but nothing moved. We were silent for a time, holding each other. Weeping. Then we slept again. When I awoke, I could feel Eyann shaking. I had never seen her so afraid. So uncertain. She, who was so confident. So strong. She who had taught me so much suddenly seemed very young. I had to do something. Say something.

I said, "Let us tell each other stories."

I told her the stories I had told before. The stories my mother had told to me. About her *Eschar*, her blood kin, and the stories they had told. About the floods that had drenched their far north homeland, the years without rain, and the great cold that brought hunger and death. How they had left to travel the path south, believing in a sun-lit land strewn with flowers and trees heavy with fruit. A land near water so huge that large lands were afloat upon it. A sea with waves that swallowed up the shore and fish that jumped into waiting hands. About the gatherings, the *Synkalos*, where many tribes met to trade and celebrate the Goddess, *Ge*. The man who had attacked my mother and taken her voice. The Aziri who found her, and the Zsuirai who attacked the Aziri and taken us. My mother and I.

Then I thought, "Why am I telling her these unhappy stories?"

I said, "Eyann, you talk now."

"Yes. When I was very small and someone would ask what I was called, I would say 'Atai.' This is what I would answer until I understood I was Eyann. I was not wrong. Atai is who I am. I was happy as a child. Shooting an arrow for the first time. Making a trap that would catch a small animal. Plunging my small fingers in Earth. Dropping seeds in wet soil. Proud that I could make food for my people."

She told me about the woman who had birthed her and the others who had cared for her when she was young. About a horse she had loved that had fallen and died. And her first *amayo*. Then, she became quiet.

We tried once more to move the rocks away from the entrance. It was hopeless.

I began to feel pain. My leg was hot and beginning to swell. Infected. I began to seek the healing leaves in my sack. But then I laughed. Laughed to myself. It did not matter.

There was little air and it was becoming hard to breathe.

Eyann said, "You have the leaves that bring sleep?"

"Yes."

"The ones that will take us to Earth?"

"Yes."

"Can you find them? It is so dark."

"Yes. By touch. By scent"

She said, "What shall we do?"

"We can wait. Perhaps the rain will wash the rocks away. And we can flee."

"We can shout, make noise so that someone will find us."

"The *Areia*? And kill us. Or make us *dolos*. No one can hear."

"I did not think I would come to death so young."

"Yes," I replied. "Our time together was short. Too short."

And we both wept. It was becoming even more difficult to breathe.

I said, "Eyann, you were my happiness."

"Yes," she said. "And you, mine."

"Eyann, think of *Elithe*. And I will think of *Ge*."

"But we have no birds to send our spirits to Earth."

It was I who said the words. "Yes, but we will return. Together. We will be Earth and make trees and flowers. We will be those who came before. For the others who will come after."

I did not know if this was what I believed, but I said the words. For Eyann.

I took the leaves out of my sack. The ones that caused sleep. The ones that would bring us to Earth. I put one in her mouth, another in mine.

I stroked her hair, then her face. My fingers tracing her lips.

I said, "Come, sleep."

We drew close, lying side by side. My leg between hers. Lips touching. Breathing in her scent. Breath intermingled.

And slept.

PART THREE

PART THREE ⚜ CHAPTER 8

HOME

Another Lesvos.

Leila had just spotted her luggage when she saw her. She had planned to take a taxi home, but there was Rachel. Smiling.

"You look exhausted."

"I am. And not just from the flight."

"Come. My car is right outside. Unless it's towed."

Once in the car, they hugged. Kissed.

Leila said, "I have a lot to tell you."

"I know. But don't say anything yet. Let's get you to the house. Open a bottle of wine, and then we'll talk."

Once they arrived home, Leila showered, changed into pajamas, and went into the living room. Her favorite red wine, cheese, and crackers on a table near the sofa.

Rachel looked at her. "Feel better now?"

"Much better. You don't know what it means to have a hot shower. And a shower curtain so you don't have to mop up the floor."

"Move closer. Tell me everything."

"The good news? Or the bad?"

"Both, of course."

"Okay. You know that everything found in Greece belongs to Greece. It's called cultural property. The local councils in charge of antiquities, the Minister of Culture, other officials. They make all the decisions on archeological findings. And Greece is poor. Austerity. That means they need to keep a close eye on expenses. Like forensic testing and transporting artifacts and skeletal remains. I can't tell you how many people I've talked to. Council people. Ministry people."

"What did they say about the women in the cave? The skeletons?"

"Not much. The people I met with just kept discussing expenses. Easier than talking about two women embracing each other. I called the Archeological Institute, hoping that they would mediate. That they would intervene. Recommend that the skeletons be transported to a museum in Volos. Call in forensics. Maybe arrange an exhibit. Publish the findings in their journal. Anything. But the people I spoke to just hedged. Dependent on the Minister of Culture for excavation permits and everything else. They're not going to make waves. But I'll call back. There are other people I can speak to. Then, I went back to the local council."

"And?"

"There's more."

"What?"

"It hit the newspapers. In all the big cities. Athens. Thessaloniki. Iraklion. Probably the smaller towns as well. Excavation findings are big news in Greece."

"You? You called them?"

"No. Not me. I think word got out and some Pelion hotel owner thought it would be great for tourism and called a reporter. And the reporter contacted the Ministry and someone talked. Everyone has cousins in Greece. But what happens next, I don't know. A locked gate has been installed and the skeletons are safe. And I was told the entrance will be enlarged. So people can see in."

"Leila, you were the one who found them. You should be so proud."

"I am proud. Finding those skeletons in a cave. Women who probably lived in one of the Pelion settlements. Maybe seven thousand years ago. But I told you how strange it was. Especially, when I first got to the Pelion. It was so familiar. Like I knew the land. Then when I found the skeletons, I just felt so sad. So unbelievably sad. Like mourning. So hard to understand. I will go back to Greece. But not yet."

Rachel hugged her. "Leave me again? But listen. This is great news. Forget museums."

"Great news? Forget museums?"

"Yes. Forget museums. Let them stay in the cave. Think of it. Hundreds of women. Maybe more. Women, lesbians traveling to the Pelion to see them."

Leila looked at her. "You're being funny."

"No. I'm not being funny. Listen. Once word gets out, your hotel owner will be very happy. At least, for a while. Like Lesvos. Another Greek nightmare. The Pelion can be another mecca. Another Lesvos. Here, drink your wine. Let's toast."

Leila lifted her glass, laughing, and said, "Rachel, you're amazing. You're crazy. I can't believe it. The Pelion?"

"Yes. The Pelion. And here's to you. And here's to another Lesvos."

EPILOGUE

Someone will remember us, even in another time.

— Sappho, 6th century BCE

They fled. Those, who followed the shoreline north, rode their horses through what would become Macedonia. Then, further to Thrace and the Thermadon River near the Black Sea. Others moved their boats east across the Aegean, stopping at many islands. Naming villages after leaders in battle. Mytilene. Myrina. And further. To what would be Anatolia. Still others fled south to an even greater sea with large lands floating upon it. Thera, later Santorini. And Crete. And then even further to the hot, hot lands that would become North Africa.

Hundreds of cold times passed and there were many lies. Lies that became myths. One told how they would burn off their right breast in order to better shoot arrows and throw spears. Another, that they would betray their sister warriors by running off with men. Still another named their leaders queens. They had no queens. Only women who planned battles and fought bravely.

They fought many wars with the *Areia*—who became the Mycenaeans. And won many battles. But lost others. Like Troy. And much of what they had believed was good became bad. Desire with rules.

Then, there was no escape. Only north. And so they fled north and the people they had fought, now the Hellenes, Greeks, made sculptures that celebrated their defeat—changing ancient stories to make their Goddesses foolish. Inventing heroes and male gods. And so they rode north, then further north. And north again. Until they found home.

ACKNOWLEDGEMENTS

There are many people to thank.

Judy Grahn for her poem, "Beauty, sleeping (Who shall wake us)" published in the *The Queen of Wands* (1982). And Monique Wittig for *Les Guérillères* (1971).

A special thanks to Rowena Winick, Pam Shea, Kathy Holmes, Sarah Lee, and my niece, Betsy Melamed for their encouragement and reading early drafts. To Chloe Karl, Donna Fleisher, and Betti Viereck, my long-time wonderful friends, for reading later drafts and great conversations on women, goddesses, and matrilineal culture.

Sue Katz for her generous help in understanding the editing process and how to publish. Artist, Mardi Reed for her sketches of Amazons. Susanna Sturgis for story editing and Susan Griffin, who read every line of my manuscript—correcting spelling errors and bad grammar—and helping to improve both the story—and my writing. Thanks to artist, Greg Spalenko (gspalenko.com) for consenting to use his painting of an Amazon on the cover of my book. And especially Sara Yager, my amazing graphic designer, for her endless patience and creating both the cover and interior of my book.

Ellen Levy for finding Sara Yager. And for fascinating talks on the challenge of writing fiction and publishing. To Alice Fisher and George Thomson for encouragement and laughter when I thought I could not bear to write another draft.

And finally, the women of the International Women's Studies Institute (a women's travel organization). Especially Daphne Amit, Lily Cincone, Mara Keller, and Ellen Boneparth (the former director who encouraged me to write a final chapter). Great friends and companions as we journeyed throughout Greece, Turkey, Australia, and other countries. The inspiration for *Where There are Mountains*.

And of course, Gloria Charles—who, if she had been Tolstoy's wife—*War and Peace* would never have been written.

Made in the USA
Monee, IL
04 March 2020